Wait

at

Woods' Edge

stories by

JOHN PERRYMAN

STEPHEN F. AUSTIN STATE UNIVERSITY PRESS

©2021 by Stephen F. Austin State University Press

Stephen F. Austin State University Press
P.O. Box 13007 SFA Station
Nacogdoches, Texas 75962

Publication Manager: Kimberly Verhines
Distributed by Texas A&M Consortium
Cover Image: B. Jones
www.tamupress.com
Printed in the United States of America

ISBN: 978-1-62288-409-4

For Hemphills and Perrymans and friends everywhere. . .

Sing a new song.
Paul Hewson

CONTENTS

Wait at Woods' Edge

A tale for children of all ages…

Dinosaur Valley State Park - July 3, 6:55 am…

At dawn, the feathered god appeared silently at woods' edge, cocked its head as if in pleased recognition of the witness of the young girl—who alone of all the people at the park had seen his emergence—smiled, and then disappeared back into the dim purple shadows from which he'd come. The little girl returned her attention and earnest effort to the small dam she'd built in the eddied pool of the slow-moving river, which was really no more than a glorified creek. Unfazed by her witness. Not knowing it a witness…

Ten weeks earlier…

The bus driver for Glen Rose Elementary School slammed on the brakes on CR 204 as the inexplicable dashed across the road and disappeared into the scrub brush of a cedar brake. The children cheered and laughed and roared uncontrollably as if watching an early morning cartoon, not realizing the impossibility of what had just occurred. A Jurassic incursion into their routine commute to school. A terrible collision inexplicably avoided. A scattering and loss of young lives somehow miraculously averted. Once the bus had come to a complete stop, but while the driver was still hyperventilating and cursing his feathered antagonist beneath his breath, seven children gathered in rapt attention at the window bank on the driver side of the bus, as if before a big screen television, dancing and waving their arms as the wake of cedar branches returned to a primordial still, concealing all evidence of the creature's recent appearance, much as a placid sea

settles to shroud the breach of a vanished whale. Seven children wildly cheered and stomped their feet as if the strange beast were a local
hero done good. Only one girl watched silently. And smiled.

July 3, 8:15 am...

The water in the tiny pool had stilled, sediment settling to the
bottom of the oddly shaped bowl, which bore more than a passing
resemblance to an enormous footprint. Feet in the shallow pool, the
pigtailed girl stuck her hand in the water, index finger reaching out to
a minnow that darted across from side to side of the earthen basin.
A wind rippled the pool's surface, and the girl looked out across the
sandy, shallow river bottom around her, where the Paluxy gently rolled
passed her and toward Glen Rose some two miles downstream. Several
families with small children were exploring the riverbed, whose waters
only deepened in the channel on the west side of the stream. One
old man, smoking a pipe and wearing Jack Lord shades and Bermuda
shorts, awkwardly wielded a metal detector on the far bank, occasionally bending down to pick up something, examine it, and either deposit
it in his pocket or discard it. Behind her, at the campsite they'd reached
the previous afternoon and that looked out on the shallow waters, her
grandparents sat beneath the awning of their tiny trailer, working dili-
gently to light a grill and spray on sun screen, all the while occasionally
hollering out instructions: "Be careful!" and "Keep your hat on!" and
"We love ya!" They had been especially anxious since they'd learned
that morning, while waiting in line to use the latrine, that they'd slept
through a slight tremor in the early hours of the morning, an unheard
of geological event in this part of the state until the spread of fracking
over the previous ten years. They also knew that though they themselves had slept through it, their grand-daughter most likely had not.
They had not mentioned it this morning at breakfast, but it worried
them. And made them perhaps freer with their instructions and advice
and warnings.

But the only instructions the little girl was minding at the moment
were those that had been issued by her feathered friend, who had told
her to sit quietly and wait at woods' edge.

One year earlier...

At no time had he ever stopped to consider the likelihood of his being mocked by his own livestock. Resented, perhaps. Attacked, definitely. But mocked—never. Perhaps this confidence itself was a sort of miraculous and naïve occurrence, for at one point the state registries had recorded that the population of such birds in Texas exceeded well over a million, and there was good reason to believe that even this number was low as many ranchers under-reported to avoid taxes, and so there was ample reason to assume that some such owner would eventually find himself the object of mockery. Incredibly, by the time the millennium arrived, there were many more such birds dotting the prairies and Cross Timbers of north central Texas than there were pump jacks. And though the official membership numbers in the state association had dropped precipitously in the late 1990s, the prices remained good for a breeding bird and in fact had tripled since the early years of the fad. Indeed, some breeding pairs had fetched over 50 grand on the market as area ranchers confidently proclaimed emu the new pork, microchipping their investments to protect them against modern day rustlers. More than other states, Texas was confident it would reach its goal to create a bigger, better bird, one whose every part and portion could be leveraged for profit—monetized by modern industry—creating a veritable feathered revenue stream for the bold investor: thighs for steakhouses, oil for arthritis and eczema, and eggs so large that a single crack of a shell could produce an omelet whose equal would require six yolks of a lesser bird. But even with these uses, the emu was doomed.

For every booming market must suffer a correction. And due to the overexcitement of some and the fraudulent practices of others, the market crashed. Mortgages were lost, college funds dried up, life savings disappeared. The dream of the gentleman rancher, breeding emus like Angus or Hereford, vanished. Bottomed out. Tens of thousands of birds were simply let loose form their pens out of despair. Other ranchers paid to have their beasts euthanized or emptied their .38s into the foreheads of their birds while they were folded over in sleep. Four months earlier, one despairing rancher, whose wife had recently left him and who would later turn to driving the local elementary school bus to pay his mortgage, killed most of his herd with his Mossberg, and then when it jammed, he took his old Louisville Slugger to the birds, later confessing to a friend that "Braining an emu is like trying to hit a baseball at the end of a slinky." But the executions had not all gone well.

As he sought to corner his prized bird in his feeding pen, each staring the other down, the earth began to tremble beneath his feet as a fracking quake struck. The rumbling seemed to pull the earth out from under him, and he fell to the ground just in time to see his fence poles shake and sink, his 14 gauge steel wire mesh sagging—eight feet becoming four—as the emu vaulted the obstacle in an awkward yet athletic maneuver that astonished the rancher and made him stop in his tracks and admire the atavistic beast he had so recently wanted to brain, almost— but not quite—bringing to his conscious mind the notion that he'd just witnessed a sort of strange grace.

Though he was pretty sure man had not lived while the dinosaurs roamed, he couldn't help but think that a dinosaur was indeed roaming while man lived. But his speculation subsided and his fury quickly returned as he watched his investment disappear into the woods to the east, headed toward the power plant at Comanche Peak. And after he'd lifted himself off the ground, and dusted off his jeans, he muttered to himself—"Go on, stupid bird! Can't even fly…What sort of bird is that? No real bird!"

Fortunately, he'd put his guns away, dragged the several feathered corpses into his barn, and for the most part collected himself by the time Sheriff Troy Wells arrived. A worried neighbor had phoned in a complaint in the midst of all the gunfire. "Though truthfully none too fond of the recent city transplant who always wore a Cox Business School cap and a Keep Austin Weird t-shirt, he had lately grown especially worried about his neighbor's mounting number of eccentricities: rebuilding a new truck engine, carrying around a bottle in a brown bag, and scouring the countryside with a metal detector. For his part, the emu rancher thought his nosy neighbor a knuckle-dragging Neo-Con. Sheriff Troy knew none of this history, only that he had to respond and make an appearance, even though he didn't really want to investigate." He just wanted to fill out some paperwork and cover his ass. And by the time his cruiser was pulling off the long caliche driveway and back on to Highway 67, the emu was miles away in the thick of the Cross Timbers.

July 3, 9:53 am…

After she'd finished playing in the shallow pool, she returned to the campsite, where her grandmother waited for her with a thick terry cloth towel, wrapping her in its folds and hugging her dry. "There ya go, dear. Love ya good, girl!" The tiny form curled up in the embrace of her grandmother's arms, and as her grandfather swatted at mosquitos and tried to light the grill, she thought back on the events of the previous night. She'd awakened with the tremor, and slowly sat up in the dinette they converted each night into a cramped bed. Once certain her grandparents remained fast asleep in their bed, she opened the trailer door and sat on the threshold.

There was a full moon, and the light playfully reflected upon the slow-moving stream situated just below the campsite. On the far shoreline, an impossible form, Seussian in shape, stood straight and motionless. It cackled softly, then disappeared into the cedar behind it. And she stood up, crossed the shallow riverbed, and followed. She picked her way though a hundred yards of cedar and mesquite, beyond a meadow and a copse of post oak, through another cedar brake or two, and finally down a slight incline toward the bank of a broad creek. From the shoreline, she gazed out into the stream's center, where an enormous shelf of rock had just erupted through the earth's crust and was now visible for the first time in millions of years, still smoldering from its sudden and recent journey through space and time. The scars and assorted markings on its tableau defied the wisdom of the wise and every other category of knowledge known to man. Seemed the lost hieroglyphs of a forgotten tongue. She smiled. Her friend cackled and leapt upon the ledge, strutting across it in a quirky gait that resembled nothing so much as a jig, and then jumped down into the shallow stream before her. She smiled again, waved goodbye, and headed back to the campsite.

Though she did not realize the complex implications of what had been revealed to her, she sensed it was important. But what she could only intuit, adults would soon confirm. The vague wording of 19th century land deeds and the imprecise nature of that earlier era's surveying instruments would be only part of the problem. And now that the predicament was compounded by the altered path of the riverbed due to the drilling-induced earthquake, the county assessor and other assorted experts would face an unprecedented quandary, eventually determining that the Jurassic Rosetta Stone existed in a sort of terra incognito, an archaeological limbo, and that Austin would have to decide which landowner on which side of the stream—the frack-happy, creationist rancher or the left-wing personal injury lawyer-turned-organic-farmer—had the better claim to the sliver of real estate whose interpretation would now determine much. Would determine, some insisted, everything.

She could not know any of this. And wiggling free from her grandmother's embrace to return to her little pool, she did not even know that her friend had been causing a stir all across the county for the past several months. In the last week alone, the emu had been spotted gesticulating wildly in the Morgan Mill tabernacle, eating computer innards in an E-Recycle trailer parked in the lot of the First Baptist Church, marking its territory on the Somervell County Courthouse steps, furiously rounding the bases on the Glen Rose High School softball field, and digging up Sheriff Troy's asparagus bed. She squatted down in the pool and cupped her palms together, catching the minnow in her handheld world, and gazing at its slender form. She dropped her hands to the basin and then splashed the waters and giggled. Then she wiggled her feet and tried to poke the minnow with her big toe and giggled some more. She was blissfully unaware of any charges accumulating on the rap sheet of her new friend. And as she dropped herself completely into the waterfilled footprint in the Paluxy, her grandfather looked up for the first time in ten minutes and called out to her that the grill was now lit and that—"Hallelujah!"—they'd be having hamburgers for lunch.

One week earlier...

"Honey, I caught her on the porch at sunrise again. Staring into the distance. That's the third time this week. Why do you suppose she does that?"

"You know why. The doctor told us."

"No, I don't know why. What the doctor said made absolutely no sense."

"It was what you said that time on accident. Without meaning it."

"I didn't say anything."

"You did. I know you didn't mean it. But you did. And you only got yourself to blame," he said, regretting his choice of words just as soon as he'd said them.

"I most assuredly do *not* have myself to blame."

"I didn't mean it that way—I meant... if she hadn't overheard you that time talking about how she got stuck in the birth canal she'd be out running and playing with the other kids. Problem is she still thinks she's stuck. And that that's why Janie died in childbirth. She thinks it makes her closer to her Mama. Thinks it can bring her back."

"And like I told you then, that's the dumbest explanation I've ever heard. That doctor's a quack, and you're a fool to believe her."

He was silent.

"You *don't* believe her, do you?" she asked.

"Suit yourself."

"You oughta have more faith in your wife. Be more supportive." She was frowning.

"I'm plenty supportive. You're my angel."

Both were silent for a good while.

"Well, I wish whatever it is, she'd hurry up and get unstuck. Makes me nervous, being up early like that. And all alone."

He remained silent, thinking.

"Was it too much to give her my Medic Alert necklace? Will that only make it tougher for her with the kids? I feel like I might have been crowding her. Was I crowding her?"

"I think it's all right. She seemed to believe it was a locket of some sort."

"I don't want her stuck her whole life. I want her to be independent. To spread her wings and fly. More than anything. That and be happy."

"Take a miracle to unstick her now. But miracles occur."

"Then we'd better start prayin'."

"It's tough on a youngster to learn that who you thought was your Mama ain't your Mama."

"I guess so."

"No guessin' about it. But there's only so much we could have done. Once Billy ran off... We've done all we could. And you've been the most loving mother she could have ever hoped for." He reached out and touched her on the arm. The truth was that they'd both probably spent more quality time with their grand-daughter than they ever had with their daughter. "Don't be too hard on yourself. It was only a matter of time. She would've figured it out eventually. All the other kids' Mamas are half your age."

"Our age."

"Hmm?"

"*Our* age."

"Oh, yes—*our* age. Sorry—suit yourself. Still, it's a tough way to learn the person you thought was your Mama ain't your Mama."

"I guess so."

"We gotta keep her busy. That's the thing. Provide her with excitement and distractions. Learning opportunities. We'll go camping next week and get her mind off things. I'll call up Dinosaur Valley this afternoon. Book reservations. That'll get her mind off things."

"I'm not sure her mind's ever *on* things."

"Take her canoeing. Go to that safari place—Fossil Rim. Have some picnics. Grill some burgers."

"I'm worried, Clint. ... I think we may need to take her to some specialist or something I know that might sound drastic. I know the school didn't think it was necessary. And that Ruthie and Paul aren't for it. Does that sound too drastic?"

"No, it doesn't. But you're preachin' to the choir."

She bit her lip and paused for a moment, then tilted her head. "I think you might be misusing that expression."

"Hmm?"

"Nothing... After all these years, though, I'm starting to fear there is no choir. That there's never been one. That there's nothing to choir for." He sensed her sudden change in tone and took her hand in his.

"There's a choir for everything, hon. And we'll make it through this. Get her through it, too. Promise. These things generally sort themselves out of their own accord. In the fullness of time. Worrying about it ain't going to speed it along."

"There you go again. I don't think you're using that expression the right way."

"Now's not the time for such things. Don't you worry none. We just got to keep her from having those fits."

But the fits continued. They'd begun in earnest when she'd learned in first grade that the town she'd been born in, Meridian, was where the annual rainfall average plummets, literally straddling meteorological worlds. Soon after, she combined that knowledge with the fact her birthday fell near the winter solstice and at the end of a decade on the edge of the millennium, and it only got worse. No matter what they tried to tell her. No matter what the doctor told them.

And the solitary vigils at dusk and dawn continued, too. Every day. She sat so still, and for so long, that she registered wavelengths lost on others. At night she woke before storms broke and ran not to her grandparents' bed but to the threshold of her room, where she hugged the lintel until morning. She could smell her cat's cancer a month before he died, and two weeks before the vet's diagnosis, she'd dug a hole for him in the garden before her grandparents knew what was what. And a few months later, when she dug a really big hole in the backyard, both were quick to schedule their annual physicals and beyond relieved to see her lining the hole with a tarp one day and trying to make her own wading pool. But their concern grew again when one morning they noticed strange tracks around the little pool. Bird-like tracks, too big for wild turkey. Tracks with three toes.

July 3, 12:27 pm...

She quietly ate her hamburger without saying a word. She wouldn't join them on the picnic table, preferring to sit on the steps of the trailer, torso leaning against the doorframe. She'd done it at breakfast, too, and they were tired of arguing with her and let her do as she wanted. But when she finished, she ran over to her grandmother and gave her a hug and a kiss on the cheek and then did the same to her grandfather. They politely told her it was nap time. Though she wasn't particularly tired, she went into the trailer as expected and laid down on the dinette bed. But all the while the tiny, pigtailed portal was thinking about the bird at woods' edge.

One hundred and fifty years earlier...

The same cedar brakes that hid the escape of the prized emu and concealed the domed cooling stations of the nuclear power plant had provided Comanche cover for their forays into the Cross Timbers area as they probed frontier defenses and attacked small mill communities like Barnard's on the Paluxy in the years before the Civil War. Not long after, when the town had been renamed Glen Rose, the turmoil of Reconstruction descended upon the hills, with disputes over land titles and conflicts between scalawags and old soldiers who came at night in sheets. A whole new variety of unpleasant legal records accumulated, leading more than one courthouse to go up in flames, including Granbury's in 1875. Then mounting tensions with newcomers, like the blood-feud between the Mitchells and Truitts, would burn bright for years to come. Soon after, the local waters gained a certain notoriety for their medicinal qualities, and tourists flocked to area hotels to seek miracle cures.

Saloons and sanatoriums thrived at the edge of what would soon be known as the whiskey woods. For not a generation later, the cedar and post oak and blackjack that covered the rocky hills provided excellent cover for the bootleggers and moonshiners who, during Prohibition, constructed stills by creeks that meandered through the area, far from the trails and eyesight of snooping lawmen but near enough the parched throats of Fort Worth and Dallas to make them a profit, rivaled only by the cedar post market for yearly revenue. This dangerous local industry was brought to an end by the events surrounding the violent murder of a key witness in the early 1920s and the Rangers' subsequent arrest of forty locals, including the county sheriff and attorney, acts that discouraged illegal activity in the years before the amendment's reversal.

But incredibly, one cottage industry seemed to lead to another with the creative and endlessly hopeful denizens of the region, and soon dinosaur tracks were discovered on several area ranches. And then in the lower Paluxy near Glen Rose. And at the height of the Depression, the tracks were dug up, boxed, and sold to generate income, less to attack Darwin and more to pay mortgages. And it was hardly an hour's hike through the timber so thick it had often discouraged the Comanche from their mischief that the nuclear plant would be built and that an ingenious if problematic way to extract natural gas from earth's crust was pioneered, the latest in man's creative attempts to monetize the natural resources of the area. But though the stills were abandoned and largely forgotten, and the fracking seemed destined for a similar fate, the footprints remained.

July 3, 5:30 pm…

And it was one such footprint that the little girl now resumed playing in. She'd had the afternoon nap that her grandparents insisted she take—more for their own recovery than her own, she knew—and was ready to assume her post in the riverbed. She sank her body down into the entire footprint, as if it were a sort of natural tub, and though the water didn't go up much above her waist, it felt cool and refreshing. She smiled as she saw the minnow remerge around her feet and once more she wiggled her toes at it.

"Watch out for snakes, Bellvania!" her grandmother called, less trying to frighten her than express care for her. "It's getting near dusk and this is when they like to come out and chase little girls about!" She waved at her grandmother and gave two thumbs up. "Love ya, honey! Love ya good, now!" she yelled out to her, to which Bellvania responded with a heart hands and a big smile her grandmother could not see.

Bellvania didn't much like her name, and most of her Palo Pinto schoolmates knew why, being as she was named after a notorious roadhouse one town over. Her mother thought it would be fun to name her only child after the tavern she'd sneaked into as a kid and which her mother had sneaked into before her. Though most everyone in the county knew of the roadhouse, most no one knew how to spell it. And this caused Bellvania tremendous embarrassment. If she'd only been given a middle name, she would have gone by it. But she was only Bellvania Jones. And the name didn't lend itself to shortening or a cute nickname. Bellvania didn't want to go by the name *Belle* because she hated the tinny clank of the school bell, and she didn't want to go by *Vany* because the thought of blood made her sick. So it was Bellvania, which meant there was constant embarrassment and confusion any time roll was called or Valentines distributed. Though she was tempted to change her name, she wanted to honor her mother's selection. This dilemma had, in part, driven her into the five-year silence from which she had not yet emerged. A silence which other kids made fun of and which had limited her circle of close friends to exactly zero. A silence about which her grandparents, as loving as they were, remained in partial denial. As if to refute the problem, her grandmother called out once more to her, just to let her know she was not alone even though they were giving her space. And Bellvania smiled and waved her hand again.

At that same moment, in the campsite office on the other side of the park, Sheriff Troy had arrived and was questioning visitors. The park manager had called to report that several early rising campers had seen another bird going through the dumpster and scattering trash all about the campsite loop, though he himself suspected it was coyotes. He was getting tired of it and was seriously mulling over just staying up one night with his Glock and a silencer and putting an end to the problem, but he decided better on it and had called in his old high school buddy once more. Sheriff Troy was tired of such calls, too, yet he was also tired of his asparagus getting eaten, and he was about of the mind that if he had a chance to shoot the bird he would, SPCA be damned. He took out his little notepad, dated the entry, and stepped up to interview the first camper in line, a quirky character in an SMU cap, Bermudas, and thick framed shades that he was sure he'd met someplace before.

Summer of 1908…

Perhaps not surprisingly, it had been a great flood that revealed the footprints, and a pimply faced kid every bit as unlikely as the goatherd discoverer of the Dead Sea Scrolls who had stumbled upon them one summer day in 1908, while hiking alone along the Wheeler Branch right above where it empties into the Paluxy. A Glen Rose schoolteacher confidently identified them as dinosaur tracks, but few local eyebrows were immediately raised and exactly none was impressed. Two years later, Charlie Moss and his brother Grady were fishing in the same stream when they, too, stumbled upon tracks, impressions they were certain belonged to a giant. It wasn't long before Jim Ryals started chiseling the tracks out of the riverbed, boxing them in makeshift wooden crates, and selling them for meager profit during the Depression, beginning what was most assuredly one of the more curious lines of work to emerge

from Somervell or any other county in the early twentieth century. Incredibly, the boxed tracks were spotted at a general store in New Mex-
ico by a paleontologist working for the American Museum of Natural
History, and the debate was on, as scientists and creationists briefly performed a sort of awkward reenactment of the Scopes Trial of only a few
years before. By the time the Panzers rolled into Poland, the WPA was
involved in the matter, and the heavy hand of the federal government
was weighing in on proclaiming and preserving truth, determining that
there were indeed dinosaur tracks in the region but that the human track
was likely a diminished metatarsal impression from the same creature.
Something like a consensus had arisen, despite the construction of a
creationist museum along the banks of the Paluxy, and a sort of detente
established. But heretofore all lines of argument in the debate had centered on ancient tracks, not on living dinosaurs. But the heretofore had
not experienced the arrival of Bellvania Jones.

July 3, 7:17 pm…

By the time dusk was approaching, Sheriff Troy had patiently made
his way around much of the campground and was interviewing an older couple at site 17, just four spaces away from Bellvania's tiny trailer.
Hovering strangely just beyond their conversation stood the man in the
Bermudas with his metal detector and a brand new permit dangling from
a bright red lanyard, trying to appear as inconspicuous as a man in rural
Texas can while wielding a metal detector, wearing Bermudas, and sport-
ing a bright red lanyard. None suspected that his fortunes had recently
turned and that he was now living, and not merely camping, at the park.
For her part, Bellvania was now dancing around the water-filled hole,
using a stick she'd recently found to playfully poke about a frog she'd
dropped in the footprint a half hour earlier, and then finally lowering
herself into the pool. Her grandparents watched form a distance, shaking
their heads with amusement.

"Isn't she a sight?" she asked her husband, chuckling. Then, becoming a bit more serious: "Honey, you heard about that emu over in
Morgan Mill?"

"The one dancing around in the tabernacle?"

"Mmm hmm."

"Yeah. What about it?"

"Well, what'd you think?"

"I don't know. What do you mean?"

"I mean…"

"I think Paul's actually the one reported it. He's been trying to track down the last of those birds. For over a year. I say *birds*. Gotta be more than one. He wouldn't lie. Even though that critter's been getting at his peach trees for the past year."

"Oh, I believe him and all. I mean, what do *you think*?"

"Stop speaking in riddles, woman."

"I mean, you know, Jesus and a dinosaur and all…Under the same roof."

"Hadn't thought about it like that before."

"Well…"

"Well…why not, I guess? A tabernacle's just a fancy word for a big tent, right? And you're supposed to fit a lot in there. Anyhow, the way I learned it, he broke bread with tax collectors and sinners and all sorts of folks…"

"Hmm…" She looked away. Not fully satisfied with his response. "You *know* what I mean."

"I mean, why not? There was one at the manger, after all."

She snapped her head back and stared at him. "Clinton Henry!"

He winked at her. "Just kidding. There weren't one at the manger. Just one on the ark."

And at that exact moment, Bellvania screamed with delight as the minnow had squirted out of her cupped hands and into her lap, causing her to jiggle her way out of the water-filled footprint and come running excitedly across the riverbed and toward her grandparents. They smiled at each other. Both knowing it had less to do with each other than with the beauty of the exhausting and freckled mystery they'd received into their midst in their old age. Their eleventh hour chance at redemption.

She stopped halfway between the footprint and their campsite and waved at her grandparents, who waved back.

"You can stay out a bit more, Love! Supper ain't ready yet. We'll call you in when we're all set."

She jumped up in the air laughing and ran back to her waterhole. Sinking into its cool depth, she glanced back once, and then carefully took off the odd locket her grandmother had given her, folding it up in her shirt next to the hole.

Forty years earlier...

For some time, the Paluxy River Valley was filled with the curious, believer and unbeliever alike. It was not until the informal field work of Glen Kuban and Tim Bartholomew that some of the tracks resembling human impressions were proven to be merely the result of erosion or sediment fill that inevitably occurs over millions of years. Most figured that once the findings had been published, the days of the contrarian Deluge Society were numbered. Though some of the controversy had been manufactured and manipulated amid the opening salvos of the culture-war conflict, much was the result of honest misunderstanding and limited training. Later work at the Alfred West Site seemed to verify Kuban's hypotheses about the metatarsal tracks. Kyle Davies, a paleontologist from Austin, confirmed that secondary sediment can often become trapped in such prints and harden over time, compromising the original print. Additional research involving dinosaur locomotion and track color distinction evidence seemed to solidify the case that all the tracks in the Paluxy were indeed generated by dinosaurs and not a human hunter stalking behind a brontosaurus or mammoth. Which, as far as most tourists to the region and native inhabitants were concerned, made the tracks no less fantastic. No less beautiful a work of Providence. No less a different sort of miracle.

July 3, 8:11 pm...

By the time Sheriff Troy reached their campsite, Clint was putting the steaks on the grill. Though he was glad to see his old friend, he was a bit stressed trying to answer questions while simultaneously keeping an eye on the steaks and Bellvania, who was uncharacteristically particular about how well-done she liked her filets.

"Well, I suppose y'all heard our little friend's been at it again," Sheriff Troy began.

"Yeah, we heard. There was trash all over the other side of the loop this morning. And then we heard he's been out on the playing fields tearing things up. The mound and basepaths, both."

"And my asparagus beds, too!" Sheriff Troy added with some levity.

"We'd heard that, also. Just so long as he doesn't get at the okra."

"Isn't that the truth. Well listen, let me know if y'all see him again. This fella over here," he said, turning his shoulders and nodding toward the man with the metal detector who had once more placed himself within earshot, "thinks he'll be back. He's the one first reported him a while back. Said he's been digging through the trash at his place out by Glass for months. Says he loves the smell of beef and likes rummaging through veggies like the sort people use for fixings on hamburgers and things. Where lots of insects and little critters gather. Call me up if you see him. Not that I know exactly what I'll do. I mean, I got some rope in my car. And a taser. I can lasso him or something. I don't much want to kill a bird. Though I've thought about it. Lord, sometimes I can't believe what my job has come to…"

"Well, maybe you can just let it be."

"Believe me, Nina, I'd love to. But there has been a lot of property damage. I'm afraid that's no longer an option. We gotta do something. It's the part of the job I hate the most, though. Gotta tell ya."

"Well, how about we start by suing the fellow who let the beast loose. Or who bought him to begin with. I could have told folks twenty years ago that it was a fool's errand if anyone had bothered to ask. Biggest scam I've ever heard of. Folks oughta be ashamed of themselves."

"Folks oughta be a lot of things. We'll never find that fellow, though, I'm afraid. He's probably moved three counties over by now. Or he's in Vail. Or Taos. Probably Taos. Who knows? In truth, those birds were being bred all over the state. All over. I'll tell you, though, Animal Control from Fort Worth has been absolutely no help. With resources. Advice. Nothing. And all the vets around here are busy as all get out, what with all the new reports of Hoof and Mouth in Erath."

"I say we just let the thing be. The coyotes might even take care of it."

"Well, I don't know…"

"It'll sort itself out in the long run, I bet. Usually does."

But before Sheriff Troy could respond, a familiar cackle rang out across the river bottom, and all turned their heads to see its source and caught sight of the back end of an emu disappearing into a cedar brake on the far side of the stream, with Bellvania following close behind.

And they were off, with Sheriff Troy in the lead, then Nina and Clint, still in his apron and still wielding his spatula. And right behind him, the man in Bermudas with his metal detector. And they followed Bellvania through the woods, picking their way through a hundred yards of cedar and mesquite, beyond a meadow and passed a copse of post oak, and then through another cedar brake or two, and finally down a slight incline toward the bank of a broad creek. At the shoreline, the four gathered in the last light of dusk and stopped to collect their breaths, exhausted but standing rapt with attention before the inexplicable. Only after a half minute of slow recovery and careful squinting did they become fully aware of what confronted them, boldly rising out of the center of the stream: an enormous shelf of rock, still steaming from the eons spent miles deep in magma, had recently erupted through the earth's crust and was now visible for the first time since the dawn of time.

And above it, disappearing toward the sliver of vanishing sun, a by-now familiar shape seemed to have taken flight. Years later, these very different people would all claim to have witnessed something eerily similar and altogether unaccountable: the flight of the flightless bird, now little more than a dot on a fading horizon, and on its back, a tiny pigtailed form, silhouetted against the dusk, waving its hand.

"Love ya good, Granny! Love ya good!"

Today...

And though much time has come and gone, some locals still maintain that on quiet nights in the fall, the mocking cackle of the flightless bird can still be heard ringing throughout certain portions of the Paluxy River Valley, as if a vanished deity were playing a cosmic joke on the most anxious of apes, hiding a new and ancientdispensation in plain sight, suggesting that man and dinosaur and gods had in some strange way coexisted from the start, were somehow bound together in an amber instant for all of time. Forever united in the strife that divides.

A Little Reckoning

"'THE HELL I WILL.' That was it. That was all Jim said. Can you believe it?" the old man asked. His listener shook his head in disbelief.

"Me neither. I wouldn't believe it if I hadn't been there. Vance backed up a bit and tried another approach. Trying to be diplomatic and give his friend a chance to cool down or reconsider. But Jim wasn't having any of it. Vance was a bit thrown, but he hid it with that poker face of his. He told me later he'd never heard Jim speak to him like that. Never. And I have to confess, I was a little surprised myself. Not just because Jim is the most agreeable man I know, and Vance is his boss and all. But some folks is hard to read. And Jim's one of them. Doesn't have a sense of humor on some things. Not when the kids are involved, anyhow. But even if Vance was in the wrong, you don't do him that way. Jim sure shouldn't. No, sir."

"Anyhow, like I say, I was a little shook up. Jim may be iron-willed and all but he ain't disrespectful, and he's never been a troublemaker. You know what I mean? So like I was saying, I was caught off guard. But not that Vance. He's a cool customer. Even though half the Dairy Queen was now looking at us, Vance played it off like it was no big deal. Like that's the response he was expecting. I mean, here Jim is, Vance's best foreman, and he's telling his boss 'No.' But that Vance is too good, he's just too damn much."

"'I know, I know,' Vance said, kind of playful, trying to settle Jim down but still get the point across. He just smiled real big and quietly gestured us toward the booth in the back, looking for a little more privacy. Once we got seated, he continued, in a softer voice. 'It's all right to look after your boy, Jim. That's a good thing. And I would never ask you to do something to hurt Dutchy. I love that boy like he was one of my own. But here you can help him out just a little. You know, the way I helped you out just a little. And all for the greater good. Let's be reasonable men.' And he started to smile real big again and talk in that playful tone of his that you know is really dead serious. 'Think of this as your civic duty, Jim, your chance to give back since you won the Booster Club Lottery. That was a mighty big contest. I know lots of folks that'd kill to be working the chains for the game. And Hal here'll be working them with you.'"

"I nodded a 'yes.' What could I say really? Jim wasn't having none of it and started shaking his head from side to side, though still not looking Vance in the eye."

But Vance was relentless. "'You'll only be helping out the town, Jim. And you might be saving folks some heartache. Think of it as part of being a good booster. We're not asking much. Just be willing to move the chains a bit here or there. Depending on whose got the ball. Just a smidgen. No harm done. Probably won't even come to that. Our boys are good. Best team we've had in years. You just got to be willing. Willing to help out the boys, Jim. They've worked mighty hard. And now it's time for all hands on deck. Time for everyone to play their part. We don't want to cheat them out of what they've earned.'"

"'Think of all that hard work they've put in since early August. Since spring ball, really. But this summer in particular. That was the hottest summer we've had in years. Did you know I couldn't get a single day of fishing in at the lake? Had to go all the way over to Caddo to find any water. And I only got over there, what, maybe two or three times, and once was with Duane and you and Dutchy. But we caught some pretty good fish that day, didn't we Jim? And how about that bass Dutchy caught? Biggest I've seen in years. I'm talking trophy. That boy showed us a thing or two. You know, I still got a couple of filets back home in the deep freeze. And that picture of the four of us together on the dock.... Got that framed and on my desk. That's a keeper. Anyhow, I guess I shouldn't complain about the drought, 'cause I heard as bad as we got it, Odessa got it even worse. Margie's sister's from Odessa. She said they had a full-fledged drought. Had a burn ban in effect all summer. All damn summer. Lawns were dying. Hell, they even closed down the city parks.'"

"'Anyhow, look Jim,' he finally says, and I can tell by this point he wants to wind things down—'I guess what I'm trying to say is this ain't

about me or you. Never has been. It's about the kids. The kids, Jim.
Gotta think about the big picture. We can help out the team, the town,
and help Dutchy toward that school mark. Just be willing to help, Jim,
that's all we're asking. At least be willing to think about it. Would you
do that? For me—as a friend?'"

"Jim was silent for a good minute, then spoke up. I can't recall it
word for word, but I remember the gist of it."

"'Vance, I don't know what to say,' he started. 'I owe you so much. I
appreciate all you've done for me and my family. But I think if that's your
bigger picture, then I'm not you're man. It's just…I'm surprised…That's
all…I'm surprised. Where's your faith? Our boys can take Daingerfield. They're more talented than you give 'em credit for. And besides,
Dutchy'll hit that mark. Hard as he's worked, he'll get those yards. He'll
get what's earned. And he'll get it on his own, too. He's my boy after
all, ain't he? No, I tell you what, he'll get there himself without anyone's
help. I'm not gonna cheapen his hard work. No way, Vance, no way. I
know you meant no harm with what you said. But I can't be a part of
that. It's wrong. And what if we got caught… I just can't do it. Be damned
if I'd do it. I'm sorry. Y'all'll have to excuse me…'"

"And that was that. He just up and left the D.Q. Didn't even touch
his fries. Damndest conversation I've ever heard. Couldn't believe it.
But Vance is a good man, quick to forgive and all. And Jim, me and
him are still friends and all. He was just nervous 'cause this is such a big
week. He wants Dutchy to do so good so bad. I guess I can understand.
Don't get me wrong. I respect the man. He's a good father to those
kids and all. Good father. We're still friends—had a few beers last
weekend. But I wish we'd have known where he was at before we made
the lottery decision. Anyhow, Vance and me didn't want to get him
riled up or nothing. Not in public. I'm just scared we don't have much
a chance in the playoffs 'less Dutchy plays good. Daingerfield is tough
as ever. Maybe even tougher. Anyhow, ain't that story somethin'?"

"That story's somethin'." The other old man said. He was the only
customer left in the Barber Shop. All the others had gone home for the
day. "I thought that boy was on board with the program."

"I thought so, too. It's crazy's what it is. Crazy. Jim means well and
all. I guess he's just not there yet. But I tell you what, his boy can scoot."

"He's quick, I reckon."

"Yes indeed, that damn boy can scoot. But here's the thing. He's not just quick—he's like a water bug. He'll break a tackle, stop on a dime, then skitter back across the field like a... like a tumbleweed or something, blowin' and goin' this way and that. He's about the size of a damn tumbleweed, too. Other teams can hardly see him lined up behind Duane. Duane's nearly as tall as Vance now. And what is he, six two, six three...?"

"I'd say so. At least."

"But that Dutchy, he's pesky. Tough, too. I'm here to tell you, there ain't no defense against that type of speed or change in direction. You can't teach stuff like that. You're either born with it or you ain't. And in nearly fifty years of watching high-school football, I ain't never seen the likes of him."

"He's sudden, alright."

"Yes, he is. Sudden. And there's not too much of that handed out at birth. It's not every day you bump into sudden. When it appears on the scene, you tend to remember. Plus, he's tough as a pine knot and a respectable boy, too. Lillie told me he even won the school spelling bee two years ago. Wouldn't it be something to be young again, be fast as all get out and have your memory back, never forget nothin'. Not your wife's birthday, your bank number. Nothing. Hell, last week I tried to deposit a check, and I'd forgot my damn account number. Teller looked at me like I was an idiot. Like I was having a senior moment, which I guess I was. But I don't want the whole town to know it. Damn, it all, what I wouldn't give to be young again. Have another crack at it all, one last time. Anyhow, that Dutchy, he won that bee and advanced to state. Ain't that something?"

"That boy's something'. Where can we get more like 'em?"

"Wish I knew. Coach does too. Fine boy, good boy. Jim and June raised him up right. Jim's a good man. Just skittish and all. He'll come around. He already has in some ways."

"He'll come around. You're right, though, about that Dutchy. He's somethin'. They got any others comin' up?"

"Matter of fact they do. Another boy. Jimmy. Five or six years younger than Dutchy."

"That right?"

"Mmm hmm."

"He quick like his big brother?"

"I bet so. Things tend to run in the family."

"They're good folks, aren't they?"

"Yes, indeed. I tell ya, Jim's been bringin' both the boys in here since they moved to town. Jimmy and Dutchy'd follow Jim around in little hard hats like they was going out to the rig with their daddy. You've never seen two look up to their daddy more than those boys. I remember when Dutchy weren't no bigger than a minute. Hell, half a minute. Truth of the matter is he ain't grown much since. But damn that boy can fly."

"Minute's plenty big."

"That's the truth. Jim and the boys have been coming in here to get their haircuts for some time now. First Saturday of each month. June'll drop the little girl off for her cheer lessons over at the elementary school in the morning, then head on out to the J.C. for her own classes. Accounting, I think. She's something else with those kids, too. Hell, you'd think by looking at her she was still a high school cheerleader. She ain't aged a day in years. She graduated a year or two behind my oldest in, I don't know, '61? '62?"

"That so?"

"Mmm hmm. Anyhow, all them kids are good. Nice as can be. Mannerable too. But that Dutchy, ooh boy, jugged lighting."

"That's right—jugged lightning."

"The kind of grandkids you'd love to have. Course you know Jim was quite a halfback in his day, too. Went to Stephen F. to play ball. Full ride. Grew up down in Lufkin. I remember hearing about him when he was in high school. Good thing he moved up here."

"Good indeed."

"Well, when you got your own oil field supply company like Vance, I guess you can pretty much find a job for the right folks."

"I guess so."

"Yes, sir. I tell you what though, all three of those kids are good kids. All of 'em. But Monroe, it's like this—there ain't no substitute for speed. Spelling and schoolwork's good and all, don't get me wrong. You got to get yourself a education. It's what I tell all the kids who come in here, especially the ball players. What I mean is, it's nice to have a quarterback who can throw, some size on the line, a coach who don't choke in the fourth quarter. But all that, that's just gravy. Sixteen-year old boys are gonna forget their plays, jump offsides, what-ever. And hell, if your quarterback don't mess up more games than he wins—if you just break even there—then you can count your blessings. Anything more, and that's just gravy."

"Yup, that's just gravy. But good gravy."

"Yes, sir, that's all fine and good, but it ain't speed. There's no substitute for speed."

"Speed don't slump."

"That's right. That's it. It don't waver or slip up. Like confidence. Or technique. Not *here one day and gone the next*. It never changes. It's always there. Always."

"Like the color of your eyes. Or a fingerprint."

"That's right. It's like a fingerprint. And his is unique. I never seen nothing like it. He'll make a damn fine college halfback, take my word on it. I heard a T.C.U. scout was already asking about him. He's gonna be a good one."

"I reckon he will."

"Yes, he will…yes, he will. He's gotta have a big one this weekend, though, don't he? Got to. One more win, Monroe. That's all. Can you believe it? Ain't that something? First time in, I don't know how long, to make the playoffs. I think Vance said thirty years. Whew. Too long. Be nice if we could whip up on Daingerfield for a change, wouldn't it? Now that's a ass whippin' I wouldn't feel too bad about handing out. We oughtta run the score up on them sons of bitches after what they done to us the last two years."

"A little reckoning never hurt no one."

"That's right. They didn't need to hang fifty on us last year. Leave the starters in past the third quarter. That's low rent."

"A ass whippin' 'd be good for 'em."

"Yes, it would. Learn 'em how to grow up and be a man. Develop a little backbone."

"This country needs more backbone."

"Yes, it does. Especially these younger folk. A little more backbone wouldn't hurt this generation. Their daddies and granddaddies had it in spades."

"Can't take Guadalcanal without backbone."

"That's right. Iwo Jima neither. Some of these young uns think marching around in protests or taking over a dean's office is something big. Like Normandy. Or landing on the moon. They need a come uppance."

"Ain't that the truth."

"At any rate, a win'd be something. Some sort of good news. Anything to get our minds off this Watergate mess."

"Amen to that."

The one old man whisked the hair off the back of the other's neck. The man in the chair stood up, turned to the other, and handed him a five-dollar bill.

"Keep it all, Hal."

"Why, thank you, sir. Will do. You have a nice day now, Monroe."

"You too. And I'll look for you Friday night in the stands."

"Well," Hal said, fingering the five-dollar bill, "I tell you what, why don't you just meet Jerry and Frank and me over at Vance's house that afternoon. About four o'clock. Vance was gonna have some beers on ice and smoke some cabrito. Always does before the Daingerfield game. Some boys from the country club were gonna help him out. We were thinking of heading out to the field about six thirty."

"Now there's an idea."

"Yes, sir. And Vance smokes up the best cabrito in town. Gets up about 4:30 to get the fire going. Made his own smoker out of all those surplus parts he's got lying around the shop. Looks like some sort of Doomsday machine, but it smokes the best damn brisket I ever had. Makes Choice taste like Prime. Tenderest thing you've ever eaten. You can eat it with a spoon. And the cabrito's even better than the brisket."

"That a fact?"

"Best in town. He's a magician with that smoke. A real wizard."

"That right?"

"Yes, sir. The only drawback's you'll have to wash up real good to get the smell of smoke off you. Wash your clothes a few times, too. But it's worth it. We'll see you at four then?"

"Four o'clock sharp."

"Whatcha say now Barrington!"

"Let's go Billygoats!"

"How 'bout them Billygoats!"

~~~~~

THAT SAME AFTERNOON ACROSS TOWN at the practice field, Dutchy Hinshaw—barely fifteen years old and already the talk of town—was having a tough day. He didn't quite realize how much was riding on Friday night. He had even less an idea that he'd been the topic of conversation at the barber shop all week long. But early indications were Dutchy, all hundred and forty seven pounds dripping wet, was more than up to the task. He'd rushed for a hundred and sixty-seven yards against Hooks's stout line the previous week, and nine-hundred and five for the season. What's more, he'd only played two and a half quarters against Hooks and less than that against DeKalb. But as much as it would have upset his legion of followers to know this, Dutchy had more important things than the Daingerfield Tigers on his mind this Thursday afternoon. The problem had begun the night before, and its effects, the immediate manifestation of which was his fumbling pitchouts all practice long, weren't going away any time soon.

"Dutchy, what the hell's the matter with you?" coach hollered.

"Sorry, sir. It's nothin'. Jammed my thumb yesterday helpin' my dad work on his truck. Having a hard time holding on to the ball."

"I'll say. But why don't you think less about trucks and more about Daingerfield, 'cause after the Hooks' game, you can rest assured they're gonna be thinkin' 'bout Dutchy Hinshaw. They ain't gonna care none about you hurtin' your damn thumb. Stop thinkin' 'bout that truck son, and start thinkin' 'bout Duane's pitchouts."

"Yes, sir."

"And another thing," coach screamed, now addressing the whole team, who, truth be told, had been having a sluggish practice ever since the girl's volleyball team had come out to the track fifteen minutes earlier to run laps, "why don't all y'all forget that damn math test to-morrow, too. I done spoke to Ms. Thompson. We reached an under-standing. Test's been moved to Monday. Besides, you got a bigger test Friday night."

Dutchy bit his lip and looked off into the distance, thought he could barely make out a blond ponytail bobbing amid a pack of girls rounding the far curve of the track. He nodded his head at coach's words—knew what coach said was true. The whole team knew it was true.

~~~~~

BUT IN TRUTH DUTCHY'S THUMB wasn't the problem, and he hadn't really been thinking about the algebra test or even the girls' vol-leyball team. He wasn't even thinking about the playoff berth that rode

on the Daingerfield game or the possible moment in the spotlight that
would come if he set the school rushing mark. He was thinking instead
about his dad. About his mom. About a lot of things that he'd been trying to sort out. And mainly about how last night, when his folks were
gone to the school PTA meeting, Mary Kate and little Jimmy took to
playing hide and seek. And how around about eight o'clock Mary Kate
came banging on Dutchy's door, and he could tell something wasn't
right and that she'd been crying.

"What's the matter Mary Kate?" Dutchy asked, his mind still racing around about the note Lucy Alworth had passed him in history
class that afternoon asking him to meet her Friday night after the game.
It was her yearbook picture which had lain open before him on his bed
and which he'd just barely had time to close and tuck away under the
pillow before his sister entered.

"Dutch, I'm scared," she said, looking up at her big brother and
then, he thought, toward the pillow.

"Why, Mary Kate, what's the matter? Are you alright?" he asked,
trying to take his mind off the picture of Duane and Lucy in last year's
Homecoming Court while going over to Mary Kate to get her to sit
down on the side of his bed. She seemed a little distracted to him. He
patted her back gently with one hand and edged the pillow over more
with the other. Her feet dangled down far above the floor. She clutched
a stuffed doll against her chest.

"I'm scared, Dutchy. I can't find Jimmy."

"What do you mean you can't find Jimmy?"

"We was playin' hide and seek Dutchy, 'cause mommy and daddy
was gone at the meeting. They said to not watch t.v. but play some
fun game instead. So we played checkers, and Jimmy kept beating me
and then he said let's play hide and seek and he found me real quick
Dutchy, and then he went to hide. I can't find him, Dutchy, and now
I got scared."

"Well, where do you think he hid Mary Kate? I'll help you find
him."

"Will you Dutchy? But I'm scared. I think he ran away."

"Oh, Mary Kate, he didn't run away. Trust me. There's nowhere to
run to, no how. The town's just too small. He's here somewhere. Trust
me." Dutchy nodded his head and smiled, then shook his little sister's
foot and tickled it a bit. "Now where do you think he's hidin' out?"

But the five-year old was silent, her eyes remaining fixed on the floor. She was terrified and little tears welled up in her eyes. Dutchy could tell something was very wrong.

"Mary Kate, what's the matter? Tell me what's the matter, we'll find him out alright. Don't you worry none. It'll be o.k., you'll see." Dutchy brushed back her damp bangs and then put his arm around her shoulder. "Now, come on, Mary Kate, I promise I'll help you. Honest. I'll make it all better. Where do you think we should start?" Mary Kate wiped her eyes and felt a little more courage with her big brother there.

"Dutchy, I think he went and hid in mommy and daddy's room."

Dutchy was a little shocked. Their room was off limits, and all the kids knew that. It had been off limits ever since they'd moved to Barrington, which was right before when Jimmy was born and when his dad got his new job. Dutchy's mind raced. He thought of ways he might help his little brother out in this predicament. There was little doubt in his mind that Jimmy would receive a whipping when his folks found out. Dutchy tried hard to think of some solution to the problem. Nothing suggested itself.

"Dutchy, Jimmy shouldn't be hiding in there, should he?"

"No, Mary Kate, he shouldn't," he said, thinking back to when his folks first made the place off limits and how they made it clear that since the new house had a playroom there was no need to go horsing around everywhere. "He should know better than to be back there," Dutchy said. "If he messes somethin' up they're gonna be real mad 'cause that's why they don't want us back there in the first place."

Mary Kate started crying. "Oh Dutchy, Jimmy's in trouble. Jimmy's gonna get himself a spanking." She loved both her brothers a lot. She'd seen what a spanking involved and didn't want them hurt. Dutchy kept thinking of some way to help. A few minutes passed. Nothing sprang to mind. After another minute, he finally decided to speak up.

"No Mary Kate, don't you worry a bit," Dutchy said, thinking his solution out loud. "Jimmy ain't gonna be in no trouble Mary Kate, and do you know why?" She looked up confused but hopeful by his tone of voice, her tears momentarily ceasing. "Because we ain't gonna tell 'em," and he leaned over and tickled her some more with his right hand. She giggled this time and rolled back on the bed and stomped her feet in excitement. He edged the pillow over one last little bit with his left hand and then finally stopped tickling her, and she sprang back up grinning.

"You mean we don't have to tell mommy and daddy?"

"Well, I guess not. Not if it's gonna cause a big stink and all. And it's Jimmy's first time doing this. He's a good boy. Just messed up this once. But you'd better promise me never to tell no one. Never." She nodded her head.

"It's our secret, ok?"

"But aren't secrets bad?"

"Not if they keep from hurting people, Mary Kate." She was silent. "Do you understand? This is *our* secret. And that means you always gotta keep it, ok? Can you keep it?"

She nodded her head again.

"Good. Now when I say you gotta keep it, you *gotta* keep it. *Always.* Not just for a week or two. But always. And always means always."

She nodded her head once more.

"O.K.? You sure you got it? We're in this together, now. Repeat after me. How long do you have to keep it?"

"Always," she answered.

"O.K., good. Now hush up, Mary Kate, and let's go find Jimmy. Mom and dad said they'd be home at nine. And you two are supposed to be asleep by then. This is *our* secret. No one else's."

She nodded her head, smiling and bouncing up and down with the excitement of somehow being on equal terms with her big brother. He took her hand and they took off for their parents' room, Mary Kate anxiously pattering along at her brother's side, her ponytail, which had hung lifeless before, now swinging along from side to side. Though Dutchy was happy to have helped cheer up his little sister, he couldn't account for the complete change in her disposition: the sobbing frightened child of two minutes ago was now bounding along at his side. She couldn't contain herself. For his part, Dutchy was a little less enthusiastic, and he started for a moment when he caught sight of something out of the corner of his eye, only to realize it was just himself, vaguely reflected on the surface of some of the pictures, plaques, and framed diplomas which lined the dim hallway leading back to his parents' room.

She giggled out loud when Dutchy lifted the bed cover and screamed in mock fear as he looked underneath. "You're silly Dutchy," she grinned. They looked in the bathroom next, under the sink and then behind the rocking chair. Then Dutchy spoke up real loud, trying his best to sound grown up like his dad. "James Vance Hinshaw! If you don't come out here this instant, I'm either gonna tell mom and dad on you when they get home, or…" he paused for effect, winking at his little sister who grabbed his hand and squeezed it with delight, "or else Mary Kate and me are gonna go eat all your Pop Tarts. And all the Blue Bell, too."

They heard a high pitched and muffled giggle from their dad's closet. They tip toed up to the door and listened. The rustling of clothes convinced them that here was what they sought. Dutchy nodded at Mary Kate, and she smiled really big, the doll she still clutched in her left hand now swinging back and forth. Dutchy threw open the closet door and heard more clothes rustling in Jimmy's retreat to the far corner of the dark space. Dutchy sorted through the clothes to the back. Mary Kate was bouncing up and down next to him in anticipation of finding Jimmy and from excitement of being somewhere she knew she wasn't supposed to be. Dutchy peeled back the last bit of clothes and revealed Jimmy, huddled in a giggling mass at the furthest possible place in the closet.

"Why, what do you suppose we got here, Mary Kate?" He nudged the squirming body with the toe of his house shoe. "Why looky here, Mary Kate, it's Jimmy," Dutchy said, still holding back the clothes, shaking his head and almost ready to laugh himself at the pathetic spectacle of his brother curled up like a frightened pup.

Mary Kate giggled and shouted out, "Looky here Dutchy, looky who we found out! Gotcha Jimmy, gotcha! Now you find me!" and she ran off with a cackling Jimmy in hot pursuit.

But Dutchy stayed put, and looked closer at the big coat Jimmy had been hiding behind, the white coat which lay partially folded back across his right forearm and which he presently allowed to unfold, causing it to hiss like shook flame. He stood stark still for a minute and looked really close and saw it was no coat, and it also wasn't the monogrammed bathrobe that his dad got when he joined the country club when they'd moved to town and sometimes wore around the house on Sundays. Neither was it his mother's wedding dress, which is what he thought it must be next, figuring that since she had so many clothes now her closet was probably full and all. But it was no wedding dress which he'd curtained back to reveal Jimmy. It was a big white hooded sheet.

He had the sudden sensation of being in free fall. Utterly alone, without words or family. He reached out for the closet wall to steady himself, thinking he might hyperventilate. He couldn't account for what he saw, because his daddy was a decorated veteran and on the school board and had won an award as a Den Leader and had a plaque in the hall to prove it. And he was at a PTA meeting that night with mama and went to church each Sunday. Yet Dutchy also saw what hung plainly before his eyes. He could not move, felt fixed by the shining whiteness that seemed to have burned away all noise and time, leaving him alone in this moment—one toward which all those previous had moved, and from which all those to come would proceed.

Dutchy stood in silence for a minute until his heart stopped racing. He struggled for the right word to cross his lips, but he could manage nothing: only nodded his head and stared into the whiteness like moonlit lake. Then with the latch-click of a closing closet door, the silence was gone. He carefully resituated the bathroom, shut its door, then made sure the bedroom was in order, and finally returned to the living room, for he'd decided it was probably best he'd seen nothing. Jimmy and Mary Kate were laughing and screaming and running around the kitchen. Dutchy told them in a real calm voice there'd be no more hide and seek in their folks' bedroom, and to go brush their teeth and hop in bed and say their prayers because mom and dad would be home real soon.

He went back to his room and paced back and forth for a half hour. When his folks came in, his mom went back to his room to tell him goodnight, and he said "Goodnight" like nothing was bothering him. Then he brushed his teeth and tried to read some in his history book before going to sleep. He was having a hard time keeping his thoughts focused. Again and again, the events of the night flashed before his eyes. He was unsure of what he'd witnessed. He wondered if he'd seen it all wrong and thought about how he might secretly return to their room one day to look again and check. But he knew there was no going back. He searched in his mind for some sort of explanation. It seemed he could make sense of nothing. But before he fell asleep, he started thinking about Lucy again, and he felt less bad thinking about her now than he did earlier and only this thought helped him drift off.

~~~~~

THAT FRIDAY NIGHT VANCE SERVED up his cabrito, and the
Billygoats played host to their archrivals Daingerfield. Dutchy played
really well, rushing for almost a hundred yards and scoring a touch-
down, but some remarked he didn't play as good as usual. He fell just
short of the freshman rushing mark, and the strong Daingerfield team
pulled away in the final quarter of a hard fought game. Later, when
Dutchy had showered after the game, he told his folks he wanted to go
hang out with some friends, but that he wouldn't be out too late. They
said alright, but they were worried about him after the tough loss and
decided to wait up for him. He came in about a quarter to midnight,
a little earlier than they'd been expecting. He looked tired. His mom
sat him down and cut him a slice of cake she'd made that afternoon in
expectation of a win. Jimmy and Mary Kate had even been allowed to
stay up to see their brother to try to cheer up his spirits.

Dutchy appreciated what they were all trying to do—he figured
it's what he'd be trying to do if he was a parent—but he was too tired
to say much. After a while he had some of the cake with everybody
but then he started to cry, and he couldn't stop and his folks couldn't
figure out why because he'd played real hard. And he never cried. His
dad came up and put his hand on his shoulder and brushed back some
of the hair out of his eyes. Mary Kate and Jimmy grew quiet and scared
and thought of their game of hide and seek. His mom kept asking him
what was the matter, but Dutchy just said it was nothing and continued
to cry. Though he wanted to push himself away from the table and
leave the house and go anywhere, he didn't. More than ever, he felt
bound to stay put with his family, even if nothing seemed right. Mary
Kate felt afraid and looked to Jimmy to see what they should do, but he
was now eyeing the uneaten cake. And when she turned to her mom,
she saw her fingering her watch and staring at the floor. Mary Kate
turned her attention back to Dutchy, just missed seeing the troubled
look that came upon her mom's face while she jerked her head violently aside, as if catching a whiff of smoke where smoke should not be.

Jim was confused, too, didn't know what to do, but he put his arm
around Dutchy. "Don't you ever worry 'bout nothing, Dutchy. Don't
you ever worry, you hear?" he said, patting the young man's head. "This
season's over now, son. It's finished. And you don't have nothing to be
ashamed of. You put it all on the line. Gave it your all. Your mama and
daddy love you so much. Nothing can ever change that. No spelling

The Tutor

"*HISSY FIT?* MORE LIKE A *TEMPER TANTRUM*. *Temper tantrum* has a certain... a certain gravity that *hissy fit* lacks."

"Ridiculous. You've got to be kidding."

"Quite serious, actually. *Hissy fits* are for ill-bred urchins. They're frivolous, whimsical, triggered by wounded egos and frustrated pleasure principles. *Actus Reus,* without just cause. They're a feature of the lower order mammal. *Temper tantrums* are the byproduct of civilization. They always have, as their Latin root suggests, a noble and just cause."

"Latin, my ass. And please don't give me any more of your courtroom crap. *Temper tantrums* are for pouters and whiners and spoiled brats, too. Just like *hissy fits.*"

"A *tantrum* involves a certain degree of moral indignation. Look it up in the dictionary. Besides, no child of mine throws a *hissy fit.* I won't stand for it. Not on my watch."

"Well you'd better stand for it, 'cause she just threw a *hissy fit,* didn't she Chris?"

The last thing in the world I wanted was to be drawn into such an argument. My goal, as always in such matters, was to be Switzerland. Forever neutral. I wanted to pick up my check for tutoring and get the hell out of there, but it was never that easy. Fortunately, I was spared from having to muster some vague response.

"Don't bother answering her, Chris. We both know Katie didn't throw a *hissy fit.* We know there are no *hissy fits* in my house."

"Yeah, well you're throwing one right now, Mr. Lawyer."

"Am not"

"Oh, yes you are."

"A *tantrum,* perhaps."

"A *hissy fit*, damnit," she shouted, tongue snapping like a riding crop. "A g-damned *hissy fit*. Do you hear me? *Hissy fit! Hissy fit! HISSY FIT!!!* Why don't you look it up! LOOK IT UP NOW, DAMN IT!"

Finally cowed by his wife's anger, he bowed out with a meek, "I shall," and left the dining room to the sanctuary of his study in some distant wing of the house.

Each Tuesday and Thursday afternoons, my visits to the Middlinger household were peppered with such exchanges as the parents carried on a running dialogue of insults and assorted nonsense that meandered from room to room, occasionally lingering over the dining room table where I tutored their only child from five o'clock to six thirty. Apparently, from as best as I could tell, neither parent had a fulltime job, other than insulting each other and antagonizing their nine-year-old daughter. They were some variety of Trust-a-fundians, I figured, a rare but not altogether unprecedented type in the suburbs north of Dallas.

Of course, I tried to stay out of the conflicts. But it was hard. Very hard. I'd usually grit my teeth and hunch back over the workbook with Katie until the shouting faded away into another wing of the neo-Tudor monstrosity. Though she was only nine, Katie was as embarrassed as I was. We had struck a secret bargain not to speak up during the shouting matches for fear of prolonging them or inspiring hostility in one of the combatants who might interpret our pleas for quiet as partiality toward the other parent.

In truth, I felt nothing of the sort. I thought them both insane. Thought Katie was the only sensible person in the house. I felt sorry for her. This sympathy and my insatiable hunger to pocket the ninety-dollar check I received at the end of the night kept my mouth shut. It was a strange scene, every Thursday night, but perhaps not so remarkable given the environment in which it unfolded.

~~~~~

ABOUT HALFWAY BETWEEN DALLAS and Denton, State Highway 289 crosses an upstart of a Farm to Market Road, creating a union that transformed what had recently been a lonely landscape of fields and rolling prairie into a desolate landscape of commerce, of bright satanic malls and giant gas marts, of McDonald's and Gaps and Sam's. This is a plain of cement and shiny surfaces, a prefabricated suburb where Escalades and F150s sweat and struggle, shoulder to shoulder, to claim the final slot in the mall lot, only to race home to their rear access garages, pleased at having successfully evaded any meaningful human contact. It is an endless procession. A dismal circulation. A zero sum.

Above this grayscape, on the northwest corner of this intersection, rises the grandest mall of all. A wondrous concrete keep of modern convenience and prefabricated construction, skirted by a bleached lot that provides easy access and egress. A church complete with a lobby Starbucks, a movie theater-styled marquis, smoked glass windows, and crowned at top with a cross made of steel beams that houses a cellular relay tower and appears, at certain distant angles, to be haloed by the satellite dish mounted near the rooftop generator.

Here, where hardly a generation separates Fighting Farmers from philistine philanthropists, wealth is secreted with admirable efficiency among superstores that cast a broad, low-slung shadow. Not a half mile from the Middlinger household, one can sit in the splendor of a Hadrian's-Villa-styled-steakhouse, order a hundred and fifty dollar cut, then cross the crowded lot to a busy storefront and by a pair of tires for your car that together cost half as much as the filet you just consumed. It is a bizarre juxtaposition of extravagance and economy, one whose absurdity is largely lost upon the surrounding populace. It is a world of golf courses and gated developments, where monstrous houses are squeezed onto shallow lots and sit, awkward and contorted as a hippo on a tricycle. Here, there is no respect for proportion, for yards or vistas, for the human scale, for were the dining room window open on any such house, you could practically spit from your passing car onto the plate of a diner. If you'd been granted access to the community by the guard booth. And if the family actually ate together at the dining room table.

For the concern is more with appearances, and no appearance is as strange as the hybrid style which comprises the houses themselves. A style that generally strives to mimic the grand manors of England, where each successive generation might add a new wing, a fountain, a stable onto the main structure, the variety melding together in a pleasing whole that keeps the house forever new and yet affirming its age and the passage of venerable generations. Here, the style is forced and confused. A haphazard cacophony of quotations stitched together, a bastard's blind stab at respectability. Tudor and Bauhaus. Gaslamps and astroturf. Here, the wealth was made at noon and will likely depart by dinner. Into such a community I whored myself, twice a week. Ninety bucks a trip.

If I condescend to such communities, it reveals more my bitterness than their shortcomings. For the truth of the matter was I had been outwitted by Trish Middlinger, otherwise I never would have found myself on their payroll. And I, like them—but infinitely less proficient in my pursuit—was willing to do anything for a dollar.

I should not castigate myself so much, though, for no tender graduate student of twenty-two could have ably defended himself against the nuanced and cunning rhetoric of Trish Middlinger. Though I could quote Gadamer and translate Rilke, I could not resist her tactics. But time has taught me there is no shame in this. This world is not run by Gadamers or Rilkes. This world is run by Trish Middlingers.

~~~~~

"HI, CHRIS, THIS IS TRISH Middlinger," said the bubbly voice of an aging sorority girl, "I spoke with you last fall about tutoring my daughter and you'd said you were interested but that your schedule wouldn't allow you to tutor that semester. You'd asked me to call you back in February when your schedule changed and you'd settled into a new routine. And, well anyhow, I'm just giving you a call. Susie Jenkins highly recommended you. I think when you'd phoned me you'd said your expertise was in reading and social science, and that's exactly what Katie needs help in. If you get a chance, you can reach me at 972-555-////. Thanks, and I hope to hear from you soon."

The message had caught me by surprise. It was so well conceived and delivered that I almost believed its account of the conversations that previous fall when she had called me repeatedly, and I had informed her repeatedly that I no longer tutored. Yet her message was so convincing and casual, worded so soothingly, as if she had my best interest at heart and was devoted to helping me out, that I even now remain convinced that she believed her own words. At any rate, three months can change one's needs and outlook on life. Three months can teach one humility, and as I had just unexpectedly been informed by the wise folks in Austin that I had exhausted my TA status at school, I needed to find a new source of income in a hurry.

Trish had got my number from the wife of one of my good high school friends. Susan herself tutored some since she'd quit teaching after having their first kid. She said she made good money. Better coin than she'd made as a teacher. My high school friends were always looking out for me since I was the only one foolish enough to go to grad school. They meant well. Kind of felt sorry for me. Susan had mentioned tutoring to me off the cuff at a baby shower we'd been to in September. I'd actually tutored once before—it lasted maybe three weeks—but I'd stopped because I'd found it intensely boring. I hadn't thought any more about it. Until Trish started calling.

Anyhow, it was the last thing in the world I thought I'd ever do until the Dean's Office informed me just before Christmas that they'd received new marching orders from the powers that be that I was no longer eligible to be a TA. That according to new laws passed by the Board of Regents, I would no longer be funded by the school. This pissed me off. I'd taught rhetoric for two years and done a damn good job. Grading freshman papers is not easy. In fact, teaching eighteen-year-olds who have just gotten away from home for the first time in their lives can be a nightmare. And so the school paid a legion of TAs to handle these unpleasant duties. Though I'd labored for the school for little pay, complaining bitterly about my superiors all the while, I was still hurt when they let me go. The pain was especially bad when I realized they'd be able to select any of several dozen eager and quite capable grad students to take my place. And as I'd recently broken up with my girlfriend and could no longer count on the income from her job at Urban Outfitters for a couple of free meals a week, I was in a bit of a bind. Then out of the blue, a month or so later, Trish called me back. And her sorority girl charm made me feel like I was one of the chosen.

~~~~~

"DON'T DO IT," TRISTAN SAID, "you'll never forgive yourself if you do."

I was uncertain what to make of his remark. Immediately, I sensed that he'd dismissed my interest as some sort of pathetic and irresponsible variety of adventurism. He was my best friend in graduate school, writing a thesis on American expatriates in Paris and London. He cultivated his own fantasy of exile by riding a bike everywhere he went, wearing a beret in the one-hundred-degree Texas sun, and blurting out things like, "Dubya's a flat earther!" at the most inopportune times. We always met at the Winedale on lower Greenville, where a pint of Spaten could be had for $1.50 and there wasn't enough pedestrian traffic around to threaten your pose.

To his credit, Tristan actually was a bit of a bohemian, born and raised in Austin by hippies. He knew something of alienation because his mother had run away with a neighbor's teenage son, and he'd been rejected from Rice and UT's English programs, somehow transferring to Dallas five years ago where he'd endured a love/hate relationship with the town, just like most of its natives. Unlike me, Tristan had a romantic view of grad school and was perfectly content to be a member of the educated underclass. My ambitions were less idealistic and my patterns of consumption decidedly more bourgeois. His grouse was largely against the commercial interests in Dallas, whereas I could tolerate the efficiency of all-night superstores even if their goods were produced by twelve-year-old Peruvian kids.

"Doesn't matter," I replied. "I never forgive myself for things anyhow. May as well get paid not to do it."

"Ah friend," he answered in a tone that made clear to me he hadn't wanted to engage in conversation but only wanted to lure me into listening to one of his rehearsed monologues. He paused, staring wistfully into the distance, fingering his goatee, pining dramatically, then began to parrot some intellectual curmudgeon. "It is the place that has done this to you. This atmosphere is unhealthy." He paused again, pointed out at the world beyond the tavern's windows, and continued. "Oh, Dallas, my home, you are already a telecom capital and yet hardly a great city, for no place can rightly be called such until it possesses a world-class university from which issues forth taste, wisdom, authority. Do you know, my friend, there's not a single peer-reviewed monograph on the history of our city?"

I'd heard a variation of this before and responded that universities didn't help a community since they were the places that now satisfied the American impulse to expatriate. People who taught in universities usually hated those on the outside. The way I saw it, the only real difference between Bellow and James was that one had a 401k and the other a trust fund. Both were bitter and ultimately corrosive, if undeniably brilliant. But this night I was not in the mood to engage in any argument.

"Authority…" he repeated dramatically, as if desiring to cue me in that he felt the vulgar masses resented this quality most.

"Shut up, you ass," I responded.

"I can't bear to live in a world of tear downs and pick-me-ups, ghettos and gated developments, Suburbans and sororities."

"Should I take the gig or not?"

"Ten million people. Ten million souls in north Texas and not a single good bookstore. Not a single Eliot seminar to be found. Can you imagine?"

"Tristan!"

"And did you hear that the library budget has been cut. There go our subscriptions. No more *Joyce Quarterly*. Farewell *Little Review* and *Athenaeum*, Adieu *Ploughshares*."

"Should I take the gig or not?"

"How much does it pay?"

"Sixty an hour."

"Take it."

"I was thinking I probably would."

He gazed from the streets beyond to a coaster on the table, and then ran his index finger along its edges. "Uhm, hey," he asked somewhat sheepishly, "do you think you can spot me a ten? I promise I'll get you back next week."

I nodded an ok, and he drained the Spaten.

And then the topic changed, and he began to parrot some other author, for that's what graduate students are taught to do: pose and parrot.

Two days later, I pulled my Tercel into the circular driveway of a monstrosity of a home and my short-lived tutoring career improbably resumed.

~~~~~

THAT FIRST NIGHT ON THE JOB I learned that I would not only be tutoring a precocious, scrappy young daughter, but also negotiating the straits of an insatiable and bloated Charybdis and an eloquent though cowed Scylla. I spent much of that first visit offering an account of myself to Trish Middlinger, justifying my grad school course of study, lying about my family's zip code, and exaggerating my travel experience. The first hour of the night turned into an awkward interview between Mr. and Mrs. Middlinger and me. We sat across from each other at the dining room table, with Katie at an end seat, wearing a green jersey that had "Piranhas" written on it. They spoke candidly in front of her, even when the topic concerned her personal matters. Katie seemed either oblivious or indifferent to it all, drawing a picture of Mia Hamm in a notebook she had.

"Now Chris, a friend of mine just got me a copy of the latest version of Highcroft's entrance exam. We need to get Katie ready to take that exam. I think they give it in May. That gives us, oh, nine weeks. She's not real good at math so we can get started on that tonight. Also, there are elaborate sections on analogies and grammar. So we've got to be sure she's ready for those. She doesn't test real good. Get's a little flustered, don't you honey," she said still flipping through the workbook without making an effort to establish sympathetic eye contact with her daughter, "and that makes me get a little flustered. Now did you say your Master's was in English?"

But before I could answer, Mr. Middlinger, who hadn't been able to get a word in edgewise, caught his wife's eye with a wagging finger. Apparently his cell phone had begun to vibrate during his wife's chatter. He saw the number, and then got up out of his chair to go to the next room, stopping in the threshold to ask his wife for instructions. "Trish, it's those folks again. What do you want me to tell them?"

"What folks?"

"That arts council, I think," he said fingering the meticulously well-groomed beard he maintained to give his sow-jowls the illusion of a jawline. "I bet they want donations for their production of <u>Hair</u>. What do we do?

She rolled her eyes. "Well, tell them we'll send them something."

He nodded his head dutifully and disappeared for a few seconds, apparently to do as told.

"Now, where were we Chris," she resumed, but before I could answer, Mr. Middlinger's head appeared around the corner and asked his wife, "They want to know if we want tickets to the show. Do we want tickets to the show?"

"Honey, <u>Hair</u>'s that show with those queers running around naked on stage. Tell them we'll send the money but don't want the tickets. Tell them we have a wedding or funeral to go to or something."

He nodded his head dutifully and disappeared once more. She waited for him to end the conversation so she didn't have to start and get interrupted again.

"'Love to give, hate to go'" she said to me as her husband concluded the phone call. "That's my motto, Chris."

When Mr. Middlinger had pocketed his cell phone and returned to the table, she turned to him a little perturbed and instructed, "make sure it's off, honey." He retrieved it, glanced at it, and turned it off. "I hate to go down to that part of town, anyhow," she said. "Gives me the creeps. Now, let's see, oh yeah, the Highcroft School. That's all Katie talks about. One of her friends from her church youth group goes there and loves it. Katie wants to go there so badly. And their entrance record into the Ivies has been…honey what has their percentage been, do you remember what Carol and Bill said?"

He shook his head timidly.

She frowned at him and continued, clearly disappointed that he could be of no help but apparently not surprised. "Well, they've gotten kids in regularly. We know Katie would love it there. They have a Middle School Spirit Squad. Absolute cutest uniforms you've ever seen. Did you say your cousin had worked there?" she asked, apropos nothing.

I nodded that she had worked there, though I had never mentioned this and was thrown off at how she'd known it.

"Oh, that'd be great. I bet she loved it. It's such a neat place. You'll be a big help, I bet. With your expertise and all. Anyhow, why don't you take this entrance exam home with you and look it over and you and Katie can get started on Thursday."

I nodded again, realizing the session was coming to a close and that I had still not actually gotten to speak with Katie. And more than a bit curious about how she had managed to score an actual copy of the entrance test.

Mrs. Middlinger was making out my check when she seemed to read my mind and said, without looking up from writing, "Katie, hon, say 'hello' to Mr. Miller. He's going to be your tutor from now on." But undetected by any of us, Katie had slipped out of the room and was nowhere to be seen.

~~~~~

TWO DAYS LATER I RETURNED to the Middlingers'. As I waited on the porch to be let in, the neighborhood struck me as somehow
eerie. There was no activity, though a few truncated front yards were
cluttered with brightly colored plastic ladders, slides, and crawling
tubes with thousand year half-lives. I'd observed at least a dozen unused Adirondack chairs in yards as I'd approached the Middlinger's
mansion. Their lawn placement seemed impractical, for there was
no vista to absorb, no neighbors out walking to chat up. All seemed
crudely calculated to suggest neighborly activity and the presence of
kids without the inconvenient noises and runny noses associated with
the genuine article. There was only silence. In a corner of the Middlingers' front yard, half sunk in photenias, sat an ornately constructed wooden booth with a sign that read, "Lemonade: 75 cents." On
closer inspection, I did in fact see a few balls and a bat peeking out of
the same shrubs, as if discarded in haste. The air was heavy and still.
The world seemed vacant. Abandoned.

Finally, a maid who spoke some obscure Eastern European language let me in. The rooms of the house were vast and uninhabited,
oppressed by the silence of seafloors. With a series of hand gestures,
she directed me to the dining room, where Katie sat alone on a chair
drawing, a half a dozen workbooks strewn on the tabletop in front of
her. She was wearing her soccer uniform and wristbands. Her cleated
feet dangled perpendicular to the floor, a good half-foot from the tile.
Somewhere in the distance, perhaps a dozen rooms away, voices were
barely audible, shouting at each other. I sat down next to her while
she finished her drawing. Finally, she looked up at me.

"Hi, I'm Katie," she said, confidently extending her hand for me to
shake. "Katie M. The 'M' is for Middlinger. There's another Katie on
the team, Katie T.. Only she plays defense, and I play left wing. She's
not as fast as me. I'm the fastest. Faster than any boys in my class. We
can race after you teach me. I play left wing because I am left-footed.
But I write with my right hand. See?" she said, quickly writing her name
on a sheet of paper and sliding it toward me for inspection.

Her handshake was firm, and she made good eye contact. She had
crystal blue eyes and honey brown hair, and her smile was two sizes
too big for her face.

"It's good to meet you, Katie," I replied.

"You can call me KM or Katie M.. Or Mster. I just wanted to tell you so you'd know. Middlinger is spelled M-i-d-d, two D's, some people mess up and only use one. Then l-i-n-g-e-r. It has ten letters. What are you going to teach me today?" she asked, returning her attention to doodling in her notebook.

I didn't respond. I couldn't think. I had just fallen in love.

~~~~~

TRISTAN MOCKED ME NONSTOP FOR about a week after I had related this story to him.

"So," he mused aloud, "my angst-ridden poet friend has fallen for the baby daughter of a brood of pot-bellied vulgarians. Tell me the details of this little encounter, Mr. Humbert. Tell me of your pint-sized Lolita of the prairie."

"You're a sick man, Tristan. She's nine. Not nineteen. It's ok to think a little girl's a cutie. It's possible to like someone who doesn't have an advanced degree. Who's not reading Derrida. Try it some time. It's possible. I know that's hard for your jaded sensibility to fathom, but it's true. For normal people, anyhow."

"Possible, but not likely. Yet if that helps you get through the day, Mr. Humbert, more power to you."

But it was true that she was a little doll. Smart as a whip and full of personality and spunk. I was afraid of what the cookie-cutter atmosphere of Highcroft might do to all this natural affability and creative energy. She had the qualities you never want a kid to lose, qualities that had long since vanished from the lives of anyone I regularly hung out with. In fact, she reminded me of no one so much as Mary Finian, a classmate of mine from many years ago and a legend at Mohawk Elementary School. Mary had moved to town with her four older siblings in November of our second-grade year, when her dad was transferred to work on an apparently top-secret government contract with Raytheon. She was a total tomboy, complete with strawberry blond pigtails and a face full of freckles. We never saw her again after that school year, but she'd entered local lore by winning the softball throw and half-mile run at our end of year Field Day. She was forever fixed in the minds of a dozen heartbroken boys at Mohawk as a type of childhood. Never to be forgotten.

Katie possessed something of the same intangibles. She was scrappy, a real firecracker. Yet as precocious as she was in some ways, she clearly had never heard of the Highcroft School before her mother had burned up the internet researching prep schools. It was obvious the idea of her testing for the place was the fantasy of the mother, who probably daydreamed about the access she'd gain to certain social circles. Like all of the new money north of Loop 635, she wanted to rub elbows with the established wealth of Preston Hollow and Highland Park, and she was convinced Highcroft—though an upstart, a very well-endowed upstart—could put her on something like equal footing with this crowd. Katie could have cared less about such things. All she wanted to do was play soccer and draw. I was worried.

For I knew all about the Highcroft School. My cousin had taught there several years back, and I had even substituted there for a few days during my first month in grad school. If it was Highcroft I was up against, then I had my work cut out for me. They had some of the toughest admissions' standards in the city, accepting something like one out of ten kids. Tuition would set you back twenty-five grand a kid. But the benefits were substantial. You got to mingle with the best and brightest. Students got into their first-choice colleges at an alarmingly high rate, enough to cause cross town rival St. Thomas to go into a panic and hire an additional college counselor this past year.

The Admissions Director at Highcroft was a notorious character. He supposedly kept track of how many Ivy League legacies he rejected. Posted the rejection letters on a wall, like pelts. The rumor was it got him off. He actually was very smart and accomplished, but he'd felt slighted when no Ivies came calling during his senior year of high school, and he'd been forced to major in journalism at Missouri, a great school and program but apparently lacking the designer label clout he so clearly craved. This job allowed him revenge. And he supposedly exacted it at a brutal and heartless price. I knew all about the guy. He had married my cousin the previous summer. Though there were some who would insist he could be a smartass, I knew he had a heart of gold. And if he could be a smartass, then he was our smartass. And we loved him anyway.

The funny thing was that most of the parents who were so worked up about their kid going early admission to Yale and Princeton had themselves gone to A&M or Baylor. They thought their kids would be failures if they weren't Elis or Tigers, yet the truth of the matter was that most of the parents had turned out pretty well from a financial standpoint, and there were even more than a few of them who were happy and genuinely good people, even if they regularly succumbed to the lure of Gucci and Lexus.

Yes, I knew Highcroft well. Ironically, perhaps my most memorable experience had not been the classroom side of my short visit as a sub, where I got to teach a half-dozen kids who had scored above a 1500 on their PSAT, but the unique rite of the lunchroom. Each day in the cafeteria, the Parents Association organized a team of volunteers. A brigade of the best dressed and most attractive young mothers in the Dallas suburbs dished out chicken pot pie and mashed potatoes next to older women in polyester cafe uniforms who were perhaps the most upright and fiercely loyal employees of the school but who, by the end of the day, just wanted to get off their aching feet and out of their shoes. The pimply-faced boys ogled the show from their seats and tried to go back for seconds and thirds. The teenage girls tried to overlook the competition, which was considerable.

Despite the best intentions of the Parents Association's program, and even most of the moms, who were usually very busy ladling gravy or scooping cobbler, a small handful of them seemed intent on undermining the spirit of the endeavor by viewing their assignment to serve as an opportunity to sport the latest Manolo Blahnik or Donna Karen, imagining trips to restock the salad bar with sprouts as a sort of improvised runway on which to strut before an adolescent audience. Despite the extra thirty pounds that hung about her squat frame, Trish Middlinger seemed determined to do her best to uphold the sanctity of this time-honored rite. But only if Katie got in. I knew the pressure was on.

The manner in which Trish described the situation to me one afternoon before Katie and I began our studies made the stakes especially clear. While Katie was off in the kitchen getting some Gatorade, Trish sat me down, and we had a heart to heart.

"Chris," she said, warmly pressing my forearm, "Katie and me, we have…issues. This kid is so smart. But she just doesn't want to do schoolwork. She wants to draw and read and play soccer. Just look at her, she lives in that damn uniform. I have to fight her to get her not to sleep in her cleats. Every single night it's the same routine. I could help her with her studies, but I've got so much other stuff on my plate right now. It's just a mother/daughter thing, I think. We're kind of having a hard time. It's just a phase, I'm sure, but... Do you know what I mean?"

I nodded.

"We've done everything to help her with her studies. Last summer we enrolled her in VBS and sent her to PSAT class and cheer camp, but she caused such a ruckus that the counselors called us up and made us come get her. I mean, it was only a day camp, but still. I'll never forget how embarrassing it was. She actually socked one of the other little campers just 'cause she said something about her cleats."

I could tell Trish had struggled just to get through this little bit of the story. She paused and collected herself.

"We just want the best for her. For Christmas we hired a sweet little gal from Neiman's to work with her on her wardrobe. She'd picked out the cutest pieces. Stella McCartney. Burberry. But Katie wouldn't have anything to do with it. Nothing. It was more to boost her self-esteem and get her interested in dresses. The child hasn't worn a dress in years. Finally, we gave up and just tried to get her interested in normal kid stuff. Dolls and playing house. Mike had a few of the yardmen build her a lemonade stand, and she hasn't given the thing the time of day yet. Three thousand dollars! And she won't play with it. Doesn't even acknowledge it. It's always soccer or baseball or drawing or anything except what it's supposed to be. Anyhow, it's gotten to where she resents anything I try to tell her to do. So maybe you could work with her and get her ready for the test. We've got to get her into Highcroft this year."

"I see," I managed.

"I knew you would. Well, from what I understand, and maybe you can help me with this, Highcroft adds fifteen new slots after fourth grade, so there's a good chance for next year. But for sixth, seventh and eighth, they only add something like five or six spaces. And then for ninth grade they open it back up, but it gets really competitive. Two hundred or more applications. We've got to do this now. It's our best chance. Me and Mike have talked about getting her tested and classified as ADD so she can get more time on the Admissions Test, but we just don't know what to do. What do you think?"

Katie returned from the kitchen with her Gatorade just as her mother was finishing this question, and I smiled a hello to her. She already had a little orange mustache above her upper lip. I nearly cracked up and said a silent prayer that Trish wouldn't notice before she headed out to whatever room she spent most of her day in. But she'd read my cue and turned toward her daughter.

"Hey, honey, you come right here and sit next to Chris and y'all get to work, ok?" And then, perplexed, "Oh no, Katie, you've got Gatorade all over the place." She got out a Kleenex out of her purse and grabbed Katie's chubby cheeks with her hand and started to wipe at the mustache that had formed above her daughter's mouth. Her Lee Press-On-Nails dug into her daughter's face as she scrubbed, violently shaking Katie's head from side to side. But the orange remained. And in a moment of weakness, Trish turned to me and said, "Oh just see what you can do, Chris, please," then slipped a check into my had and was gone.

~~~~~

"I KNOW A GUY WHO CAN write a thousand words on a piece of rice."

I was confused. That was not the answer I had been looking for. I tried to regroup. Did not want to appear thrown off guard by a nine-year-old, not that a nine-year-old could detect such confusion.

"Uhm, that's great Katie. That's interesting. But let's try this again, ok? Remember, these are analogies. We're looking for analogies. Let's see. All right," I said flipping through the workbook Trish had set out for me. "Here we are. 'Stingy' is to 'magnanimous' as 'meretricious' is to?"

"Have you ever seen lighthouse man? He has a candle growing out of his head. Or he superglued it to his brain." She smiled really big.

I was not getting anywhere, and in truth I hadn't been for the previous hour. Or even the previous month. She wasn't catching the drift of the exercises we were doing. Had no idea why I had been hired by her parents. Didn't realize that more than just my paycheck was at stake. Or maybe I just wasn't explaining the exercises very well. Either way, she was not responding to the assignment. In some ways it was more challenging than TA-ing my rhetoric classes had been. In my mind I was running through ways I could better explain what we were supposed to be doing and entertaining other possible modes of employment when I was once again interrupted by her as she gazed out the dining room window and into the evening sky.

"Who lights the stars when night comes?"

I looked at her and smiled. Speechless. "You know what, Katie." I finally said, copping out on her question, "let's play a little indoor soccer."

Now she smiled, for I had mentioned the one topic that could distract her from the wanderings of her imagination. The one activity for which we shared an equal passion. I could sympathize with her attachment to her cleats and uniform. Soccer had been my favorite sport at her age. She high fived me, raised the headband I'd brought her last Tuesday up above her brow, and hopped down off of the dining room chair.

"First to three wins," I said, hoping the Middlingers were out to dinner like the maid had vaguely communicated to me when I'd arrived. I am not a proud man, but I had to admit it was kind of sad that my tutoring career had been reduced to such deception and distractions. "But after this game," I said in a serious tone, "we study history, ok?"

"Ok," she answered. Damned if she didn't almost beat me. Anyhow, the ten minutes were enough to burn off some of her excess energy, and we had refocused on our work when Mrs. Middlinger entered the dining room reeking of scotch and cigarette smoke. She sat down next to Katie and watched quietly for a few minutes while I quizzed her daughter on the geography, flora, and fauna of Texas.

"Now where are the Davis Mountains?" I asked, and Katie pointed them out on the map in her textbook.

"Good job. That's right, they're in West Texas. And where are the piney woods?" Again, she quickly pointed them out.

"They sell a lot of wood out there. And they talk funny. Grandpa talks funny. We visited him last summer, and he lives right next to a lumber yard. It smells bad," she said, waving her hand across her nose as if swatting away the stink.

I commended Katie's original answer and tried to steer the conversation back to school matters. Before Katie's brief digression on her family in East Texas, I had sensed Trish was pleased with the little scene I was trying desperately to orchestrate on her behalf, and I wanted to win her complete confidence.

"All right, let's see how much you really know now. Where do the whooping cranes live?"

Katie smiled the big smile of those in the know and pointed down at the coastal plains. "Right there."

"Good job, Katie" I congratulated her, and we high fived.

"All right," I continued, "now here's a hard one. Can you tell me where the wild pigs live?"

Katie looked stumped. She studied the map. I repeated the question again, real slowly, nervous she was going to make us look bad.

"The wild pigs, Katie, what part of the state do they live in?

She stared indecisively at the map. I sensed she was beginning to panic.

"Think of Pooh Bear's friend, Piglet," I said softly, trying to ease her nerves. "If Piglet lived in Texas, what city would he live in?"

Her hand circled desperately over the map but did not lower.

"Katie, hon," said Trish, inching her chair closer to her daughter's, "where do the wild pigs live, sweetheart?"

Katie drew her hand back to her side and grimaced some.

"It's all right, love, settle down," Trish said, gazing across at me and then back to the map. "Remember when we studied this on Sunday? Remember where we said the pigs live?" Her hand settled on Katie's shoulder and her daughter tensed up.

"Well, maybe we should have a Gatorade break," I offered, "we've been going at it for nearly two straight hours."

"No, no, Katie knows this one, I'm positive. I taught her this last weekend." Her nails gripped down on Katie's shoulder, and she tried desperately to communicate the answer telepathically to her daughter, apparently trying now to gain my confidence. Katie gritted her teeth and looked down at the floor.

"Damn it, Katie, I know you know the answer. Now honey, don't waste my time. Or Mr. Miller's. Where do the wild pigs live?"

Katie had frozen up.

"She's doing it again, Chris, I swear, she's doing it to spite me. This exactly what I've been talking about. She knows the answer."

Then staring hatefully at her daughter, she repeated the question very firmly. "Quit wasting my time and tell me where the pigs are. WHERE DO THEY LIVE!?"

Katie started to wince as her mom's grip tightened on her shoulder. And then her mother exploded.

"This is what I've been talking about, Chris. The kid has no respect for me. You're gonna drive me crazy, Katie," she shouted, "is that what you want? Will that make you happy? After all the sacrifices me and daddy make for you, this is how you treat us. You know where the pigs live. We went over it a dozen times on Sunday," but Katie had curled up into a ball in her chair. And then, even louder than before, she continued. "I've worked too hard for this. I've sacrificed too much!! You take her Chris, I just can't deal with it anymore. I'm sick of it. I deserve better than this. Where are the wild pigs, Katie? ANSWER ME NOW, DAMNIT!!!"

But there was only silence. And in a second she was gone. Had rushed out of the room to some distant corner of the house to brood and smoke her cigarettes and shout at her husband. Slowly, Katie uncurled from her protective posture and, tears coming to her eyes, looked down at the map, and opened her mouth to speak.

"The wild pig just left the room."

I almost fell out of my seat.

~~~~~

THE NEXT THURSDAY, WHEN I arrived at the Middlingers' to tutor, I was greeted at the front door by Trish herself. This had never happened before, so I immediately sensed something strange was going on. The tears in her eyes and her choked up voice only confirmed my suspicions. She ushered me into the formal living room, a room I'd never seen anyone in before, and we sat down.

"Oh, Chris, I am so sorry. So very sorry."

"What's the matter? Is everything all right? No one is hurt or sick are they?"

"Oh, Hon, it's just Katie, we don't know what to do with her."

"Is she all right?" I asked, a little frightened.

"Oh, she's all right like that, but we did take her to the doctor. Got her on some new meds. We had to do something. We've decided that with two weeks left before the admissions test we need to get help from a specialist." She said this apologetically, and for the first time during my acquaintance with her I believed she revealed more vulnerability than she might have intended.

"Well, that's ok," I answered, "I was just worried she'd gotten sick or been injured or something."

"Katie's fine. It's me. Me and Mike who've been through it all. That girl is so stubborn. Anyhow, we took her to a behavior specialist and a psychologist to see if we could get her declared ADD so that she could have extra time for her test. We're petitioning Highcroft right now to see if it's all right. Our lawyer was supposed to have talked with them today," she finished as she reached into her purse and pulled out her checkbook.

That familiar gesture triggered something in my mind, and I suddenly realized what was happening. I was being terminated. Bought out. My silence was being purchased.

Trish fought back tears as she asked, "That is Chris with an "C," right?"

"Yes," I answered, a little confused but not really upset. My only concern was that Katie would have to continue to live in such an insane household.

"Chris, I knew you'd understand. There's nothing any of us could have done. We tried. Lord, knows I tried. But we think that the specialists are the way to go now. This one's worked with Highcroft for years. Knows the ropes. And we want what's best for Katie. We know you do, too. She's taken to you, you know. Talks about you all the time. But our lawyers advised we deal exclusively with the psychologist," she said as she ripped the check from the book. "I'm so glad you understand."

She stood up, and I rose as if on cue. Her face had lost all signs of sadness and become a sort of ugly mask in repose. She had resumed her position of power. She walked me toward the door, hand gently on my back, as you might guide a kid toward the classroom on a first day of school.

"Hon, we're so glad you understand. You did a great job, really. We just think we need to look elsewhere now. This is the last chance, really. Admissions gets more competitive from here on out, and we want the best for her."

She opened the door, stuffed the check in my hand, and reached out to give me a hug and then a peck on the cheek. The wet, oily seal was palpable on my face. I'd been marked. The presence of scotch hung in the air. I left the house dazed. The door slammed shut behind me. The whole final interview had taken no longer than two minutes. Even now it seems surreal. In the distance, a leaf-blower meandered across the lawns of the development, sentenced to perdition among the grayscape of spec homes. I stood and stared into the gathering twilight. With five hundred dollars in my hand.

~~~~~

TRISTAN LAUGHED HIS ASS OFF. For a good ten minutes. A small group passing by the Winedale at the moment stopped out of curiosity, then hurriedly walked on, as if they'd randomly witnessed something deeply troubling.

"You thought you were better than they! That you could beat them," he finally managed. "You actually thought you could beat them at their own game. Look, my friend, they may be vulgarians, driven like beasts by mammon, but you're still just a grad student. Forever destined to live among the ranks of that most pathetic tribe of all: the overeducated underclass. And you're a fool to underestimate them, their cunning. Condescend to them, morally or intellectually, that's fine. That's one thing. But underestimate them? That's foolish. In any contest of substance, you'd carve them up in a minute or two, but in matters like this… What were you thinking?"

I didn't really know what the hell Tristan was talking about, but I did manage to protest, "I made over a thousand bucks for a few days' work. And five hundred in two minutes, you smartass."

"Five hundred bucks," he spat out contemptuously. "Let me tell you, my friend, Trish Middlinger wipes her ass three times a morning with five-hundred-dollar bills. You've been played, my friend. A high-priced babysitter, that's what you were. They wanted to sound you out for info about your cousin. I bet you gave them her phone number, too?"

I nodded with surprise at his knowledge. He laughed with joy.

"They probably wanted another angle to work while a team of lawyers was probing the school handbook for weaknesses, concocting ways to sue their way into the community. And there were probably other tutors, as well. On Monday, Wednesday, and Friday. You were one of many. Expendable. Forgettable. And you went along with it all because you needed the cash for Starbucks or some other silly boojee addiction. Your Old Navy fetish. Your love of Chuckie Taylors. And because your nine-year-old had a cute smile and liked to kick the soccer ball around. Pathetic."

I stood motionless, in stunned defeat. He sprang upon my silence.

"Ah, good friend, I fear your education has unfit you for life in this city, for life among the vulgar. Leave now. Settle in Paris or Prague. Perhaps Rapallo. I hear it's nice this time of year. Leave, I tell you. Leave, or succumb to a world of PlayStations and Quicken. Those are your choices. But you can decide on this later. Tell me, though, loverboy—because I'm intrigued—what do you think will become of your little Lolita?"

Though this sounded like more of Tristan's confused rhetoric, I did cringe at the thought that I hadn't been the only tutor. To this day, no thought has ever troubled me more. But I was sure I knew better. Tristan was always launching off into some conspiracy theories at the slightest provocation, twisting the world to conform to his skewed vision, the parameters and proportions of which he'd absorbed from reading too much Foucault and Freud. Because grad students are essentially indentured servants with few prospects and less disposable income, its part of their psychology to invent scandal and conspiracy to add texture to their world. To pass the time between classes. How on earth he figured I'd been played, I had no idea, but my concern for Katie was real. I had to find out about her. Yet two months would pass before I found the courage to drive by the house, and by then her fate had been decided by Highcroft's Star Chamber.

As I drove through the neighborhood on that warm June afternoon, it seemed there was even less visible activity in the yards and homes than before. No doubt there was some correlation between the rising temperature and the eerie absence, but that couldn't explain the complete withdrawal of human life. Incredibly, even more faux Adirondack chairs sat around empty lawns, unused. The once brightly colored plastic toys that had lain scattered in the side lawns of a few homes were now entirely faded and drained of vigor. Several sat on a curb awaiting the weekly trash collector.

Though the guard at the neighborhood's security booth had recognized my car and waved me through, I was still nervous. My nerves turned to confusion when I rounded the corner on Katie's street and noticed an object stationed on the curb of her house's lot. As I approached, I saw to my relief the half dozen balls and bats that had become a fixture of the yard, lying around, perhaps having been recently used. But this new object at the front of the lawn overwhelmed them all. Was strange. Enormous. As unexpected as if it were an Apollo capsule. A bright yellow lemonade stand.

I drove by the house slowly, wearing my shades and a baseball cap, and saw a sight I thought I'd never behold: Katie, wearing a sundress and what seemed to be an English bonnet, sitting at the lemonade stand. She looked forlorn, miserable, completely broken in spirit, confined to the stand as if it were the stocks. My heart bled for her. She'd been reduced to a prissy, public spectacle. A bean counting stooge. I drove down to the end of the street and then turned around and tried to summon the courage to stop and buy a cup of lemonade. As I approached the house from the other direction, I noticed that the maid sat at the front window of the dining room, observing her young charge through the glass. It was just like the parents to pay someone to keep their daughter under constant surveillance as they forced her to do something against her will. No doubt they were somewhere deep within the house, pursuing each other room to room in meaningless and never-ending argument.

I parked my car in front of the house on the opposite side of the street and got out. As I approached the stand, I noticed, out of the corner of my eye, that the maid stood up out of her chair to closely eye the transaction. When I was within six feet of the stand, a vaguely familiar voice spoke up in what can best be described as an exhausted drone.

"Good day, sir. Can I interest you in a cup of Texas' best homemade lemonade? It's only seventy five cents a cup. Or two cups for a dollar. It's lemon-licious."

It was the sales-pitch of a middle-aged mom. Possessed the studied cuteness of a former sorority rush captain. Forced, desperate, defeated: it had Trish's fingerprints all over it. It was all I could do to keep from crying.

"Why, yes, I think I'd like a cup please," I managed.

We had not established eye contact yet, and I had not wanted to identify myself so as not to draw the attention of the maid, but as Katie handed me the lemonade, I looked into her crystal blue eyes, hopefully for a sign of recognition. But there was nothing.

"Keep the change," I said, handing her a dollar bill in a gesture that I hoped would break the spell. She took the crisp one very professionally, as if she'd been handling money for years, and placed it in a little lockbox.

"Thank you, sir. Come back when you can. We're open ten to two on Monday through Friday, and eleven to one on Saturdays."

It was just too much for me to take. I had to know what had happened to my spunky little firebrand.

"Katie," I whispered, trying to hold the maid, who still stood at the front window, within my peripheral vision so as to detect her possible approach. I could just make her out, hands on hips, no doubt frowning, apparently disapproving of the additional communication. "Katie, it's me, Chris. Your tutor. Remember me?" I dipped my sunglasses down on my face as proof.

I searched her eyes desperately. For something. Anything. Some sign of recognition, or a sympathetic expression of appreciation that I'd played an important role in her life. She gave me a Stepford stare. Her eyes were vacant, body-snatcher empty. My heart sank to the soles of my feet.

And then suddenly, after a half dozen seconds of silence, she spoke. And I'll never forget what she said.

"You! You're as bad as her! Even worse! At least she doesn't know any better!"

"Katie, I only wanted to help. We wanted you to go to Highcroft. To get extra time. I think you're the greatest. The brightest little girl I've ever met. Maybe we could kick the soccer ball around some time. I'll call your mother and see if it's ok." But then I'd noticed that the maid had left her perch, and the front door was opening.

As if she had eyes in the back of her head, Katie resumed her pitch. "Thanks for your business sir. Come back when you can. We're open ten to two, Mondays through Fridays. And eleven to one on Saturdays."

"Katie, I promise I'll call," I whispered, retreating to my car at the advance of the maid who had shouted some orders in a harsh language entirely foreign to my grad school experience.

"Thank you for your business, Sir. Have a nice day."

There was nothing I could do. Nothing I could say. So I left. In shame.

~~~~~

About a year later, I again summoned the courage to drive by the house. Tristan went along with me for moral support. I hadn't spoken with the Middlingers since the day of the buyout, and I had no idea what had become of Katie. I had no doubt she could get into any school, but I had doubts where she might fit in and retain her native curiosity and affability. The Highcroft crowd didn't seem her type. A familiar sense of shame came over me as we lied our way past the guardhouse. I felt as if I'd abandoned her. That whatever had become of her was my fault and mine alone. I *had* known better. There were a thousand questions and regrets running through my mind as we turned onto her street.

My questions were soon answered. As we approached the house, I was struck this time by the complete absence of balls and clutter that had once distinguished its yard. Now, but a single object could be found in the yard, and it wasn't the lemonade stand. It was much, much worse. A sign, shaped like a megaphone, was jammed into the ground outside the dining room window. Painted on it, in the bright blue and red of the Highcroft Patriots, were a pompom and the words: "Kathryn: Cheerleaders '06 Rule!"

That night, Tristan and I drove down to the Winedale and sat at the bar. For the first time, I believe he sympathized with my sadness. My oceanic grief. He bought me a few beers and after a while tried to start up conversation. It didn't work, and he soon gave up on the idea. Eventually, he wandered off to another side of the bar. Several minutes later I heard him swear and slap the pinball machine. And I began to wonder if I'd been too hard on Trish—we all seek advantage, especially for our kids. Surely that was a forgivable crime, I mused. But I was at a loss. For the rest of the night, I stared out at the grayscape beyond the tavern window, felt the burden of the gathering superstores, heard the hustle of ten million worker ants, and mourned the cancelled journals, the seminars that would never be, and all my lost loves.

The Curious Case of *The Nonsense Shadow*

"THE WORD TROUBLES YOU, AND PERHAPS—in a strange way—that is the purpose of all words, yes, Mr. Sweeney? That is their glory, the peculiar power they exert over us mere mortals. Words are unsettling. Unpredictable. As a favorite poet of mine once wrote, 'They've a temper, some of them, especially verbs,' and indeed they do. It is our duty to guard against forgetting this. But every day we take our use of words for granted, exchange them like so many coins that have lost their embossment. We neglect the sanctity of language, forsake the holy seals which stamp our words, and in the process we become estranged from their divine origin. For you see, each word is a covenant, each syllable a social contract, whose terms we can never fully appreciate."

"Even this word I used to christen this criminal, I minted it this very morning, and I fear already that it is unknown to me, has taken on a life of its own. For although the act of naming empowers one over the named, this is one act which must be attended to with the proper comportment. With humility and due reverence. Dangerous things, words. And they must needs be, for theirs is a dangerous task: to negotiate the abyss between presence and absence, to put in the place of nothing…something."

"But in this year of our Lord 1993—precisely one hundred and fifty years after the birth of the Master—our criminal would have you believe there's no bullion in the bank, nothing to back this currency of words. Would remove us from the gold standard of divine law. That is why the 'Biblionil' is the most dangerous criminal alive, why he threatens to undermine the very foundations of our civilization. And that is why, Mr. Sweeney, you must apprehend him, must put an end to this madness, once and for all. By any means necessary."

"No doubt this word of mine, this unprecedented creation, strikes you as foreign, a bit of gibberish, or even nonsense, and in a way it is absurd. For it is an absurd person who would commit such a crime. Allow me, if you will, to dissect this baroque Latinate, this disorienting, elaborate, Ciceronian compound. For this is not the crime of some reckless brute. The barbarians are not at the gate, at least not yet. No, this is the crime of a decadent. A thoroughly cultured and highly-educated man, and as such it requires the appropriate word. No rude Germanic root would suffice. No clumsy Saxon suffix. They would detract from the sophistication of the crime, would betray the machinations of a coarse sensibility. And the 'Biblionil' is without a doubt the most sophisticated of criminals, is most assuredly an aesthete. One who lives for nothing save art. And who, consequently, kills for nothing save art. This villain—this *heretic*—would make of books...nothing. Curious, is it not, to coin a word for the destroyer of words, to provide currency for these most unholy of acts? But I fear that is the only way to cast light into these shadows. The only way to beat back the dark. And there is so much dark..."

"So you see, Mr. Sweeney, this is a criminal worthy of the name I have bestowed upon him, and as perverse as you may find the case, I can assure you it disturbs me still more. This crime against humanity, against our western inheritance, is unpardonable. It haunts my sleep and casts shadows upon every minute of my day. And though history teaches us that the destruction of books by burning is not without precedent, and has occurred often in times of great social turmoil, such burnings have seldom been successful. Yet this incident is of a different cast altogether. This perpetrator, this unprecedented monster, would put all at hazard. By comparison, those previous bonfires seem like crude, pedestrian affairs. This sin is more calculated and sinister, more thorough. And totally anonymous. A cowardly act. A most foul and unnatural deed. For were we ourselves not spoken into being by words, by the very breath of God? What punishment, then, is fit for he who would destroy a book, for he who would reduce words to nothingness – to which ring of Hell, Mr. Sweeney, do we assign the 'Biblionil'?"

"I am not ...I am," Sweeney stammered, clearing his throat before continuing after a short pause, "not sure I understand."

Willingham, who had found himself well-pleased with the diction and delivery of his monologue, a speech he'd dutifully rehearsed three times that very morning, fell silent before his audience of one. He began tapping his fingers across his desktop. During the awkward silence that ensued, Willingham began to realize how thoroughly unimpressed he was with his charge, felt his eloquence lost on this large, dull man before him. He'd known after the initial contact that he was taking a chance with the hire, but he felt it was a first step that could be easily reversed, if need be. Still, he cursed himself silently for listening to the daytime manager of his dry cleaners, an octogenarian who had for years bragged about her nephew, a lieutenant with the force. Willingham had indulged her ramblings, for the cleaners were around the corner from his apartment, and he'd used them since the Johnson administration. And because, he had to admit to himself, she'd reminded him vaguely of a washerwoman from *Dubliners*. So when she'd mentioned the previous month that her nephew had taken early retirement and was beginning a new career as a security consultant and private investigator, he'd thought perhaps he'd sound out the services of this retired detective from the NYPD.

But now, as Willingham stared across the desk at Sweeney, who was violently blowing his bulbous and fleshy flushed nose into a filthy, red-checkered handkerchief, it occurred to him what the problem was: Sweeney had likely never had such close interaction with an Ivy League graduate before. And certainly not an Eli. Or rather, not an Eli of his own vintage—he caught himself in the midst of this self-flattering digression, for he knew better than any that New Haven was not the school it once had been. Who couldn't get into Yale in 1993? Once a palisade of piety and intellectual striving, the last of the Ivies to appoint a non-clergyman as President, the school was practically accepting people off the street these days. In fact, he feared it was little better than a glorified trade school, and in jest to himself, he frequently referred to it as Yale Polytech.

He'd seen the transformation firsthand when he'd been appointed an assistant professor during the first stirrings of the revolution some twenty-five years earlier, and it viscerally disturbed him to this day simply to recall the changes, the 'progressive policies,' as they were so-called: the increase in public school admits and the accompanying plummet of acceptances reserved for his dear Groton, the rise of need-blind admissions, the admission of women, and—most problematically—the controversial tenures of Brewster and Coffin, the latter of whom had actually granted an interview to *Playboy*. What self-respecting chaplain did that? All of these changes were enough to rattle a third-generation Bonesman who'd just received tenure. Even the construction of the Beinecke was tainted with a touch of scandal. More Modernist monolith than library; more fit for Kubrick's chimps than Dwight's disciples. Its design had eschewed the gothic and classical, and not even the scholarship of Pearson and Gallup (which it housed) could redeem it, nor could the gift of Supino, who'd donated his fine James Family collection to be housed at the new library. Nothing, Willingham was certain, could atone for the tasteless structure that rose in October of '63, wedged into a lot between the Law School and The Scroll and Key Tomb. And yet somehow he knew even then that the structure would be consonant with the tenure of Brewster.

With a similar degree of certainty, he'd known that the summons he received in the spring of '69 did not bode well. Presidents, even young ones such as Brewster, did not just invite junior level faculty to their chambers for a one-on-one. Still, he could not have conceived of Brewster's directive: that he drop his seminars on James and Eliot and pick up freshmen surveys teaching Hughes and Hurston, Stein and HD. He'd been devastated. But he knew, as he leaned back in the leather chair of his study, that in a strange way it had been this very series of events that had set him on a course that resulted in him sitting across from this oafish brute, hot in pursuit of James's lost masterpiece: poised at the very cusp of the greatest achievement of his life. This momentarily consoled him, made him think perhaps there was some sort of intelligent design behind the chaos. Still, if he were absolutely honest with himself, Willingham remained uncertain if he had selected the proper charge for this literary quest, when the sluggish shape pocketed the now dampened rag and resumed speaking.

"How... how can someone make a book disappear for good? Make all copies of the book vanish, like it never was? It doesn't make any sense to me. Aren't there some versions somewhere? Some master copy or something?"

"Ah, but not just any book, my good Sweeney" he said, with a patronizing air that he was sure was lost on his confederate, "a rare book. And Henry James's *Requiem for 'The Corner'* is that most rare of books. Priceless. It contained the collected American short stories of James, each

one of which dealt with Americans or was set in America. Every story
had been previously published. Every story. Except one—the *Requiem*
itself, and its peculiar history is one of the great mysteries of twentieth-
century literature. Though nearly a century old, this story has never been
properly studied. For years, scholars had lost track of its whereabouts.
I'm not convinced the notoriously understaffed archives department at
the Beinecke even knew of its existence. They most assuredly did not
understand its significance. In truth, though, I had only recently unearthed
its existence and had not yet had a chance to study it. To my considerable
knowledge, no library on earth besides the Beinecke even had a copy of
this rarest of works. There is no mention of it in the Laurence bibliography.
Nor in Supino's scholarship, and it is his donation that still comprises the
bulk of the Beinecke's James holdings. Not surprisingly, it could be found
nowhere in the library's card catalogue, either. Apparently, I alone had been
chosen to learn of its existence. Its....significance."

"I myself came upon it quite by accident, and I know the holdings
of that library as well as anyone. I was finishing up my last book and
making arrangements for research funding and a travel grant in order to
devote time to another project when knowledge of the *Requiem* was, how
would the Master put it, 'sprung' upon me. This knowledge promised
to change my life. I felt confident that a close study of it would lead to
a revaluation of James. I was on the verge of beginning such ground-
breaking research, a thesis that would alter the canon as we know it,
when the tale vanished from the library's holdings. But I jump ahead of
myself. Allow me to explain. The world of the scholar is no common
matter, is in fact a veritable labyrinth and might well confuse the uned—
the... *uninitiated*."

The thin, well-dressed man, whose economy of gesture and composed
tone of voice were of a clerical cast, stood up behind his desk and walked
over to the study's window. The single pane seemed to transpose the
study behind it upon the city before it, while framing the man within
it. Willingham had long fancied that it doubled as both a looking glass
and a window into the dark recesses of humanity below. To Sweeney, he
appeared to be collecting his thoughts in silence; to citizens below—had
any chanced to look up and been capable of judging his countenance at
a distance of some dozen stories—he would have appeared transfixed
in a moment of religious ecstasy. So Willingham liked to think, anyhow,

as he breathed in deeply and imagined his study one of Wren's glorious side-chapels. When he finally did resume speaking, he seemed to address more the streets beneath him and the dusky silhouette of Central Park beyond than the large man seated in the chair behind him, who had interpreted the lull in conversation as an opportunity to pick his nose.

"The *Requiem's* first and only printing was private and financed by James himself. In the summer of 1914, the Master discretely retained the services of a small East Sussex firm operated by an old friend. James's plans were to circulate the book among close acquaintances for feedback and then possibly sell the rights to a large trade press. An arrangement not entirely unlike his friend Henry Adams was to manage for his study of The Mont. But the printing was halted after only three weeks when the war began, and a zeppelin was spotted in the night sky above Brighton. A panic arose, and the publishing house's machinery and personnel were quickly commandeered by a munitions factory. Only fifty-seven books had been printed and bound. And when the opportunity arose to resume printing at a different location in late October of 1914, the Master was so distraught by America's reluctance to enter the war, so demoralized by the English casualties suffered at the Marne, that he renounced the *Requiem*. This terrible turn of events facilitated the suppression of the greatest secret of James's career, one that has eluded Edel and Kenner and all of the great scholars of the Master: that he desired to return to America."

"Yes, in the months preceding the war, the Master had been entertaining the idea of returning to his native country. A recently recovered letter from Adams to close friend Elizabeth Cameron explicitly states this fact: that James had mentioned to Adams in a letter now lost that the Master was prepared for repatriation. America was on the verge of reclaiming the finest writer she has ever produced. After years of exile, the greatest figure ever to have risen from the shores of the western hemisphere was poised…to *return*. The implications of this revelation were obviously considerable. Of significance to any scholar, and any American citizen for that matter. The *Requiem* anticipated this celebrated return and picks up where James had ended 'The Jolly Corner' – that haunting tale about an expatriate's return to his ancestral home to hunt down the ghost of the man he would have become had he remained stateside. But Wilson, bumbling dolt that he was—naïve son of a wayward preacher man—squelched this glorious return. And, as poor Henry lamented, civilization was plunged into the 'abyss of blood and darkness.' Of how much more value the life of an American James would have been than the lives of slain American youths I will leave for doctoral students and their dissertations to entertain. That question is not mine. I must point out to you, though, that at whichever conclusion you arrive, you must agree that the end result of Wilson's wisdom was that we lost both James and a generation of youth."

"And so it was that the Master, disillusioned by Wilson's policy and embarrassed at himself for having entertained the childish and sentimental idea of return, destroyed all the copies of the *Requiem* and asked relatives never again to mention these dashed hopes. I believe that the despair he felt over America's reluctance to aid Britain prompted the Master's eleventh hour request for English citizenship. He believed America had broken its word and forsaken holy obligations, but he was too tactful and resigned to quiet despair rather than voice his dismay in public. So considered, the destruction of the *Requiem* was more than a mere gesture. It was the most significant act of the last decade of the Master's life. More important even than his English citizenship, for the latter event would not have occurred save for the former. It was, as I will advance in my forthcoming monograph, the most important decision ever made by an American-born artist. And perhaps, indeed … *any* artist."

"And though long noted by friends for his meticulous attention to detail in matters regarding privacy, the Master, on this one occasion at least, overlooked a very important detail. He forgot about the original, hard copy of the *Requiem*. His amanuensis had succeeded in rescuing both the original version of the *Requiem* she herself typed from his dictation, and also a single carbon. Though one would have hoped she'd have saved several copies for posterity, she apparently chose not to. Her diary reveals her long inner turmoil about whether to keep, or destroy, the work. Six months after the diary first records her possession of the copy, she made an entry that confessed simply: 'Tonight I burned the *Requiem*. Henry would have wanted it thus.' Tragically, she ended her life one week later."

But fortunately for scholars, the carbon had disappeared from the amanuensis' house some time before – I personally suspect a nephew of hers who later established himself as a trifling, third-rate dealer in rare maps. Most likely, this copy was secretly auctioned on the black market, where it no doubt fetched a handsome price. As best as I can reconstruct its circuitous path, the carbon resurfaced in the sixties when a donor sold it to the Beinecke on condition of total anonymity. The vanished story has been housed there ever since, in their rare books collection under lock and key, amid acres of dusty shelves and the alleged care of a team of conservationists who, I believe, have never fully appreciated the import of what they possessed."

"For you see, in the thirty years since they came into the ownership of this manuscript, they apparently have made provisions to copy the carbon only once. *Once...* on microfilm. An unpardonable oversight. The work of irredeemable dolts. I spoke with the Director of Archives and Special Holdings soon after my discovery of this criminal neglect and was told a patchwork of pathetic excuses: that endowments struggled in the '70s due to the market's under-performance. That budgetary constraints had complicated processes. That monies got repurposed, even at schools like Yale. That some manuscripts got temporarily misplaced in the inevitable shuffle or materials between New Haven and our off-site shelving facility in Hamden. This library, possessed of so much of our western inheritance—ancient papyri, early copies of the Gospels, medieval manuscripts, Gutenberg Bibles, Shakespeare folios, the personal letters and drafts and papers of countless authors—this archive tasked with processing 15,000 new books a year and fifty feet of new manuscript per day, is not merely overmatched. It is managed by a corps of Keystone Cops. A ship of fools. And the rot, the cultural rot at its root, has a history."

"It is difficult to appreciate the damage organizations like the SDS did to legitimate scholarly undertakings and efforts at preservation. For a generation, maybe more, it distracted schools with its largely phantom political causes. Because of this and the Beinecke's fear– understandable, I might add – of being permanently relegated to second fiddle behind Harvard's James family archive, the library never acknowledged its shortcomings or mistakes and never undertook what I would consider a thorough inventory of all its Modernist acquisitions. The problem, alas, is not peculiar to Yale. This terrible set of circumstances is not so unusual in the world of rare manuscript collections, whose fates are

often determined by fools in state legislatures or wealthy benefactors
who would rather donate money for the construction of football
stadiums or cash cow Executive MBA programs than the preservation
of our western inheritance. But to think it occur to the beloved Master.
To imagine that our Henry could endure such neglect..."

"And despite my repeated letters to the Head of Printed
Acquisitions at the Beinecke, letters intending to bring to his attention
the degree to which his facility was compromising the integrity of
certain rare documents, he'd written back only once. And then to
inform me, in an endless refrain, of the budgetary restraints imposed
upon him due to the poor performance of the endowment, the lost
funding, the cutbacks in staff needed to catalogue recent acquisitions,
the reduced visiting hours, and the university's failure to purchase the
latest in conservation technology. It was clear to me he resented my
awareness of the facility's shortcomings. He knew, as I did, that it was
only a matter of time before tragedy struck. But neither of us could
have guessed how close to home it would strike."

"And in fact only when the sole carbon was found to be missing
two weeks ago – and who knows how long it had been absent since
libraries are too embarrassed to report thefts since it undermines future
attempts to acquire archives – only then did the Beinecke, after they
assured me of what had been a thorough search of the New Haven and
Hamden site, subsequently discover that the single microfilm copy had
been irretrievably damaged, most likely the result of hydrochloric acid or
some derivative, they surmised. Probably smuggled into the reading room
in a lipstick canister or a case for reading glasses. The agent of choice
for vandals intent on destroying our way of life. A not uncommon crime
against rare works of art. According to library staff, the most recent log
entries that could positively attest to the presence of the carbon version
date from eleven years back. A scholar, a professor visiting from Indiana,
apparently spent an afternoon in the Beinecke perusing the carbon. But
he died ten years ago, before he could finish his own manuscript. And
that was the only lead the library had to go on. Incredibly, they're still in
the process of entering paper records into their computer system. Paper!
In this—the 1990s! Pathetic! What records they do have indicate that,
save the deceased Hoosier, neither the microfilm nor carbon versions
had since been released to the reading room. No scholar living has

studied the work. Not even James's celebrated biographer, Leon Edel. And as for visits scheduled in the near future, only I had requested access to the late holdings of the James archives. I was to visit for a week in the early fall and had even been granted rare, unrestricted access to the entire archive. Even Wharton's silly post cards to James."

"But as I have maintained all along, I had known about the *Requiem* only for several months and would not have known about it had not a friend of mine, a scholar of the Adams clan, informed me of Henry's strange letter not long before her own, untimely death. These unusual circumstances contribute to making the existence of the *Requiem* one of the best kept archival secrets of twentieth-century literature. But of course, there are so few who are trained properly to appreciate the pleasures of the archive, so few who are willing to endure the taking of these most severe, these holiest of orders."

"So it was that Wednesday last, the Beinecke, long familiar with my time at Yale and my expertise in the fields of rare books and James studies, summoned me out of retirement to examine the damaged microfilm and confirm what they had suspected for some time. Fortunately, the Head Librarian and Provost with whom I met were sympatico, agreeing it unwise to inform the police or media just yet. For we were not entirely sure if indeed the carbon had vanished. Yale's administration knows as well as anyone that such publicity can devastate a research facility's reputation. Such bad publicity, especially in the wake of the Bass fiasco, could undermine future giving. This request for privacy, unfortunately, would be honored only a fortnight, at which time some snooping reporter from *The Times*, no doubt alerted to the theft by a leak—I suspect a graduate student working within the Acquisitions Department who had overheard some chatter—broke the story. But not enough of the story to cause a panic. And after a debriefing by the Curator of Special Holdings, and a quick tour of the archive and damaged documents, I asked them to proceed with an exhaustive inventory of their twentieth century holdings, including the James family collection, to confirm that the lost work had not been mis-shelved, accidentally by staff or intentionally by some group such as the SDS, and then to call me back a week later. Three days ago I received this call, and that afternoon I again took a train out to New Haven. And on Tuesday, at one thirty-seven in the afternoon, it was my terrible misfortune to have the task of reporting a first—the only such crime in history, I believe—for at that precise moment, Henry James' *Requiem for 'The Corner'* ceased, for all intents and purposes, to exist."

With a rhetorical flourish, the thin man turned from the window. The city had darkened beneath his watch and was now reduced to a shadow landscape and the low hum of urban activity. Countless nights before he had assumed his vigil at this same precipice, imagined his study a sort of fog-ridden rampart about which hordes gathered in the distance. But tonight there was only Sweeney. Reseating himself behind his desk, Willingham resumed.

"Only then, Mr. Sweeney, after some circumspect inquiries and careful cross-referencing, did I contact you. Your services came highly recommended. Your history with the force, and the unusual circumstances surrounding your departure, provide you an ideal resume to assist me at this stage of my investigation. We both have unique histories that, I believe, assure us we can work with one another. Productively and, of course, entirely in *confidence*."

Sweeney shifted uncomfortably in his seat and stared at the small figure before him. For at least the previous five minutes he had not been listening. This inattention was not by choice but by necessity. He had been holding in gas since the moment he'd sat down for the interview, and he was eager to expel it. Yet, with Willingham's final words, Sweeney surprisingly felt his professional reputation somehow at stake. In truth, he hadn't been aware that after his untimely departure from the force he would have enough pride in his reputation to feel it threatened. In his final conversations with Department counsel, his union lawyer had managed to salvage a portion of his pension. Thanks to a confidentiality settlement, it was agreed that the unusual set of circumstances surrounding his 'early retirement,' as he liked to call it, were not to be disclosed to the public. And it had been this sudden, unexpected change of fortune that had compelled him to pursue this new line of work to begin with. He needed some sort of regular income, especially until he was able to get his habit fully under control. The counseling required by the settlement had helped at first. But the urge was strong, distracting him, directing his attention from the racetrack to his bubbling gut when he knew he should be preparing an answer for the strange man now staring across the desk at him. He felt obligated, after Willingham's theatrics, to say something.

All he could think, though, was that Vinnie Harrigan was a son of a bitch. Vinnie couldn't pick a horse, couldn't even pick his damn nose, so why the hell should he be trusted to pick a restaurant, even an Italian one. Damn half-breed Harrigan didn't know if he was a Wop or a Paddy. He couldn't be trusted to judge cuisine. But Vinnie had insisted that Rocco's on West 68th near Central Park West served the best calzones in town, and since it was on the way to Willingham's, Sweeney thought he might grab a quick bite to eat. The gas induced by this calzone was unbearable. Sweeney felt like he was passing a knot of scalding barbed wire.

Which was unfortunate, because Sweeney had begun the day with the highest of hopes. When Willingham had told him on the phone the night before that he lived in *The Majestic*, Sweeney made a mental note to arrive at the apartment building a good hour before the interview. It was not every day one had a legitimate reason to visit the site of Vinnie *The Chin*'s attempted assassination of Frank Costello, an act which had spiraled the city into several months of historic mafia activity involving the biggest names from the most violent families. And the lobby where the attempted killing had played out was just a few floors below apartment 13J, where Lepke Buchalter of *Murder Incorporated* fame had lived for several decades. Sweeney figured he could turn his interview visit into a sort of Gangland Tour so that, if the job turned out to be of no interest, the day would not be a total loss. Out of a habit perhaps developed in his final years as a detective, when he preferred to approach crime scenes in a discreet manner, through service entrances or back doors, he had slipped past the doorman and into the lobby unseen, no easy feat for a man six foot and pushing 250 pounds. In truth, he had always possessed this talent to just appear, out of nowhere, and silently observe while remaining largely unseen. Sadly, the landlord and lobby personnel clearly did not appreciate the history *The Chin* had made in his failed effort to ice Costello, for there was no plaque in the lobby where the scene had gone down, and the 13th floor was undergoing renovation and not accessible to any but residents. So Sweeney sat in the lobby for thirty minutes, waiting to use its pay phone to call his bookie. And when the phone remained in use as his interview time was ten minutes out— and then five minutes—he abandoned hope to place his bet and headed for the stairwell for what was assuredly going to be a difficult climb, but one he was determined to make, in his effort to lose weight. He'd allowed himself just enough time to arrive punctually for his appointment with his intended.

And a bizarre interview it had been, Sweeney thought to himself as he stared back across the desk at Willingham, knowing he had to say something professional sounding. He knew he couldn't afford to appear disinterested or slow-witted. He was going to be working on a retainer, after all. This was only his fourth client since he'd handed in his badge, and he was already late with a few payments. He couldn't afford to lose a steady source of income, no matter how eccentric the client. Though he felt himself growing anxious inside, he knew his imposing size and habitual scowl hid his nerves, even if they made him appear somewhat less than cerebral. Sweeney summoned his reserves of strength, clenched his pyloric valve one last time, and spoke.

"I see, I think. Interesting case. A little out of my usual line of work —I've never really dealt with rare books—but I know some people, some well-connected people, from my time with the Blue. A buddy of mine used to work security at Sotheby's. He can snoop around. See if this thing's being talked about on the street. Look into contacts in the, er, art underworld. I got a cousin in Bridgeport, too. Works for the paper. Used to edit the Arts and Entertainment section. She might have heard some things. Or know someone who has. Her husband is an editor at St. Martin's. I'll get the word out, if you know what I mean. So I guess there isn't nothing else I need to ask right now."

"There's 'not *anything*' else to ask, you mean?"

Sweeney was silent a second, a little thrown off by Willingham's apparent repetition and tone of voice. Sweeney was unsure what to do, wondered if he'd forgotten some routine question that private detectives always asked, some standard procedure for closing down an interview. A dozen seconds passed as Sweeney thought through a number of things to ask, none of which seemed important or relevant. But he knew he must speak.

"Oh well, I guess maybe there is one other thing. Maybe it's kinda off topic, I don't know."

"Yes?"

"Well, why, if no one's reading the book and people aren't missing it— and basically no one knows it exists—why does it matter? Not why does it matter, but… if there's no market, no real demand, where's the value?"

Willingham was completely caught off guard by this question. He had no response, was even a little angry at first, but in a few seconds began to figure that it was better, given the circumstances, to have an ignorant lackey than a bright one. Yes, the question, so considered, even began to please Willingham. He had judged that Sweeney's own grudge against the law would deter him from inquiring into Willingham's motives for pursuing the *Requiem*. Indeed, that was one of the reasons he'd hired him. Given Sweeney's past, Willingham suspected he probably had carte blanche in his pursuit of the *Requiem*. Now he knew that Sweeney's intelligence would prevent any unforeseen complications, too. This was, after all, a fitting question for a former pugilist, an excop, a vulgarian whose appetite compelled him to be driven like a beast by mammon. Was not that appetite, that slavery to passion, why he had been dismissed from the force to begin with?

There is a sense of relief that accompanies one when full knowledge of the limits and inadequacies of a potential rival are unexpectedly revealed, and now Willingham felt he at last knew exactly what he was dealing with, knew the range of his hireling's mind, found it limited, almost touchingly so. There was no need to embarrass this man, he thought, no need to punch down. Better to flatter him as an equal, and in the process let him silently conclude his own inadequacy. If conclude anything at all. Willingham nodded his head, stoop up, walked over to one of the mahogany bookshelves which lined three walls of his study. He proceeded to pull down a number of books. Cradling some dozen titles in his arms, he walked back across the room and gently set them down on the desk before Sweeney.

"My only response, Mr. Sweeney, is that you read these. I dare not answer your question. That would be presumptuous of me, even foolhardy. There is no need for the witness of mere flesh and blood when the immortal words of the Master can speak for themselves. These books alone will answer your query. Read James. Let the Master testify on his own behalf."

This request disrupted the concentrated control Sweeney was exerting on his pyloric valve. He suddenly felt he should have kept silent and let his professional reputation suffer. This thought was replaced by the realization that Willingham's olfactory sense would soon detect what his auditory sense had not registered. Sweeney maintained his composure, relieved that his girth had served to muffle his wind. His thoughts returned to the case at hand and specifically to how quickly he could wind down the interview. He did not want to protest Willingham's request. At the same time, the last thing he wanted from a case was extensive research, especially when the Meadowlands opened in two days for what promised to be the most exciting racing season in years. Though he favored the thoroughbreds, his cousin had recently stirred his interest in the harness races. He was more excited for the coming season than he had been for any in recent memory. He knew his luck would change this season, just as certainly as he knew he must work to check these temptations. Each day was a battle, that had to be rewon. The war, itself, would never end. 'Not on this side of the sunshine,' his father used to say. And he preferred that understanding to the 'all things in moderation' that his union counselor had advised. But it was tough. Since his early retirement, he'd met some new people who worked down at the track. People who knew things. With so many urgent thoughts crowding his mind, he reverted to instinct and perhaps appeared a bit terse. Nodding his head, he offered, "Thanks, I've been looking for some good reading," stood up, and gathering the books in his arms, took his leave.

TWO WEEKS AFTER THIS INITIAL meeting, the first letter arrived at *The Majestic*. It was signed simply, The Nonsense Shadow. It was postmarked from Manhattan, and its message was pieced together from a variety of newsprint fonts, most likely – Willingham surmised – from a Sunday edition of *The Times*. He immediately arranged for another meeting with Sweeney, where he made him promise to inform neither the Beinecke nor the police about the letter until he himself had decided the best course of action to take. Sweeney was unimpressed with the letter. Willingham, however, was ecstatic, and even a bit flattered. He felt that in a strange way he had found a kindred spirit, for the missive informed him that The Nonsense Shadow was apparently familiar with his scholarly reputation and had learned of his involvement in the case after another *Times* article which had appeared, much to Willingham's dismay,. toward the back of the Arts section in the latest Sunday issue, mentioning only recent rumors of thefts that were circulating in the world of rare manuscripts.

The letter also related that The Nonsense Shadow was distraught by the Beinecke's inept staff and inadequate facilities and that he might even consider unloading the *Requiem* if the price were right. Were Willingham to have an interest in adding the manuscript to his own private collection, the letter related, he should take out a classified ad in the next Sunday edition of *The Times* and address it to The Nonsense Shadow. Willingham instructed Sweeney to take out such an ad, allowing Sweeney to compose the ad so as to leave no evidence of his own involvement in the case, for it was daily becoming more evident to Willingham that though his first impression of Sweeney was unfavorable, this brutish conduit could prove invaluable in dealing with what might prove to be a dangerous criminal mind. Certainly, he could now be used nicely as a scapegoat, framed as a patsy, or paid off as an alibi should matters turn for the worse. And should the plan unravel, Willingham felt confident he could maintain plausible deniability.

Sweeney said little during this second meeting, but he did survey Willingham's study, which he had been too uncomfortable to take in upon his first visit to the apartment. He had not eaten at Rocco's today, however, and he was able to appreciate his surroundings without gastro-intestinal distractions. He figured it was the kind of place where a retired English professor would live. Hardwood floors, lots of books, framed diplomas, oil paintings of several old churches, some nice – but antique – furniture. No pictures of family. No televisions. Scratchings on the arm of the chair Sweeney sat in suggested the presence of a cat in the apartment, but he was unable to verify this speculation, though a sudden but immediately vanished movement out of the corner of his eye seemed to confirm his suspicion. As did the prevalent aroma of dander and tobacco, a scent he found not entirely unpleasant and which seemed to cause his foot to begin tapping lightly on the hard wood, a movement which slightly shook the thick frame beneath the rumpled beige overcoat. Soon, a finger on the armrest accompanied the foot below. Before taking his leave with his new set of instructions, Sweeney casually asked how much a piece like the *Requiem* might command at an auction. The question seemed to please Willingham, provided him with the occasion to think aloud and hear his rich baritone resonate in the wood-paneled study.

"Interesting you should ask. I've thought about that quite a bit the past two weeks, and eventually did some research myself, finding what

I thought an astute judge of such matters would consider a comparable item. Of course. Even among experienced dealers, there can be great discrepancy. It is a subjective process. An art, not a science, as the ABAA will tell you. The condition and scarcity of the item matter greatly. So, too, the binding, the provenance, the edition. Because it is a carbon of some sort, it is especially tricky. But I would bet, depending on the knowledge of the auction house and its skill at appraisal and price inflation, it might fetch upwards of fifty thousand. Perhaps fifty-five. At any rate, I myself would gladly pay that sum for a rare James original. But how does one put a price tag on such ownership? How could one dare to reduce James to a commodity to be trafficked about by merchants? It is almost a vulgar thought, to assign dollar value, to speculate on what would be worthy of the Master's pen... But to my mind, since you ask, fifty thousand, perhaps a bit more. It's too difficult to appraise really. Of course, to me the value is really priceless. But enough of that already. You must submit an ad by tomorrow morning if it is to make this Sunday's *Times*, and I've kept you long enough as it is."

And with that he showed Sweeney to the door. Nor did Sweeney protest. The Yankees had a 7:30 start, Guidry was pitching, and in rush hour, the trip up to the Bronx would take close to an hour.

"MY DEAR MR. SWEENEY, HOW DO YOU DO?"

Sweeney recognized his employer's voice immediately, though he hadn't expected this particular call this early in the week. In fact, he had again been waiting on his bookie. He desperately wanted to place another bet before heading over to the midtown Port Authority Bus Station to catch the bus out to the Big M. He preferred the shuttle to a cab as it saved him just enough money for another hot dog and beer and the bus stop, at the intersection of Patterson Plank Road and Gotham Parkway, was a short walk to the main entrance. And though the busses were generally late, not even the prolonged exposure to the station's habitual stench of piss and sewage could kill his appetite for the Coney Island Dog he liked to eat on the apron near the eighth pole. It was a sunny day, and he was anxious to get out to the track, but he had decided to stick around his apartment waiting for the call so he could place a bet on that night's Mets' game. Gooden would be taking the mound, and Strawberry was back in the line-up. He felt sure his luck was about to turn. This game was too good to miss out on. A lot of money would be exchanging hands, and he fully expected to win big. When he picked up the phone and heard Willingham's voice, he was a bit surprised. And disappointed. He composed himself before replying.

"Pretty good," he answered, "and yourself?"

"Pretty *well*."

"Good… That's good to hear. I guess you want to arrange another meeting?"

"Yes, indeed, Mr. Sweeney. My apartment. This evening. Nine o'clock."

HOURS LATER, WILLINGHAM USHERED SWEENEY into his study and informed him that the second letter had arrived two weeks to the day after the first. It, too, like the original communiqué, had a New York City postmark. But it was the letter's tone that took Willingham back a bit, for it actually made something of a demand. Willingham didn't mind, though, for despite his protests he was secretly thrilled by the cloak-and-dagger intrigue. As he had begun to suspect, The Nonsense Shadow was not interested in destroying the *Requiem* but merely wanted to hold it hostage. For ransom. And out of respect for Willingham's lifetime of service to rare manuscripts, The Nonsense Shadow felt obligated to allow the scholar a first crack at buying the story. He did insist that Willingham not notify the police about their dealings, a request the retired professor was more than happy to honor.

It was the sum demanded for ransom that upset Willingham. He felt it unreasonable, even though Sweeney pointed out that it fell below the amount Willingham had claimed he'd pay for it. Willingham remained adamant in his disdain but had to acknowledge that fact. Sweeney offered that he felt Willingham should reconsider the demand, and that if he decided against buying back the story, it was his professional advice—based on years of experience in law enforcement—that Willingham should finally contact the FBI and share all his information about The Nonsense Shadow with them. Sweeney said he was worried this affair might escalate out of control and turn out to be a little more than either of them could handle. Willingham was indignant at Sweeney's remark. Predictably, he rejected the advice. He would have none of it and felt his intelligence slighted, as if Sweeney were suggesting his mind was not on a par with the thief's, or—worse yet—that the slow-witted detective was equating his intellect with Willingham's by referring to them collectively, thereby acknowledging that they were both vulnerable and new to this high-stakes game of intrigue.

Willingham brusquely reminded Sweeney that he was being paid "to carry out orders and not offer advice." What Willingham really wanted, however, was time. He told Sweeney to take out another ad in the Sunday *Times* demanding The Nonsense Shadow lower the price, realizing he probably wouldn't. And Sweeney did as he was told.

LIKE CLOCKWORK, THE THIRD LETTER arrived another two weeks later. Unlike the first two, though, this one made no demands. Rather, it made something of a pointed threat. The Nonsense Shadow would grant Willingham a one-month grace period to arrange for the acquisition of a loan or the necessary movement of funds, and if after a month he was not willing to pay up, the manuscript would be sold to a Japanese businessman whom The Nonsense Shadow had contacted, and who, he added, was anxious to add the *Requiem* to his growing collection of western classics, including letters of James and several drafts of the Master's early short stories. Willingham was enraged by the thought. Yet he had come to believe that the terms of The Nonsense Shadow's ransom were proof of his willingness to reach a settlement and deal in good faith. Willingham referred to it, half-jokingly, as the 'terrorist installment plan.' Sweeney didn't laugh but now insisted that Willingham contact the FBI and hand the case over to them. Willingham was even more enraged by this proposition than by the thought that some executive at a foreign firm might buy the *Requiem* as a sort of trophy of conquest.

"Three times no!" he screamed at Sweeney, "I will not be outmaneuvered by a foreign pimp. Some peddlar of Nissans or Nintendo! With no appreciation for our western inheritance. No love for the Master. They've purchased enough of Manhattan as it is. They shall not own a piece of the Master. Not on my watch. The *Requiem* will be mine! Even if I have to relent to the callous demands of my rival."

In truth, the installment plan had been thoughtfully worked out by The Nonsense Shadow. It called for a payment of $5,000 once a month for eight months, to be dropped off in a series of different locations, each of which would be identified by a phone call placed an hour before the drop time. Willingham himself allowed that it was not unreasonable, so far as blackmail went. A part of him even thought it romantic, reminiscent of a plot twist from a Bogart or Lorre movie. Still, he was clearly troubled by these recent developments. He abruptly dismissed Sweeney from the meeting, offering no further insight into his thought processes.

A WEEK PASSED BEFORE SWEENEY received another call from Willingham. The tone of his voice on the message machine was anxious, and Sweeney knew some sort of decision had been reached. Willingham had requested another meeting, and Sweeney dutifully returned the call, leaving a message that he'd be free at the appointed time in the late afternoon of the following day. So that next day, Sweeney took his usual seat in his employer's study, and Willingham shared some interesting news that might, he thought, play into their favor. Recent events had led him to believe that The Nonsense Shadow was an imposter, did not even possess the manuscript. Sweeney was stunned. Willingham, satisfied with the effect this revelation had on his lackey, proceeded to unveil his theory.

Two days earlier, Willingham had been contacted by both the Beinecke and the FBI and informed they had received communication from three different anonymous sources, each one identifying itself as the thief. The FBI immediately suspected two of the contacts were false leads. Both involved amateurish letters, and both were later followed up by phone calls from the thief himself to the office of the Beinecke's Director of Acquisitions, which had been tapped since day one. The agents succeeded in tracing both the calls. The first had come from an honor student at Manhasset High School, one of Long Island's premier schools, the precocious teenage daughter of a Suffolk County cop who had aced her AP English exam and scored a 1580 on her SAT, and the other came from a struggling writer who lived in the Village and had an extensive rap sheet, including the dubious distinction of attempting to extort money from Don Rickles by claiming to be the comedian's love child. Plans were being made to press charges against both impostors.

The FBI felt the third lead had the most promise, and in relating this portion of his story, Willingham could not contain his pleasure. Agents had informed Willingham that if he received any calls or letters from anyone claiming to be a member of the Graduate Student Liberation

Front, a sort of bastard child of the SDS, he should contact authorities immediately. Despite its absurd moniker, this organization was to be taken seriously, the agent insisted. Willingham was secretly thrilled by the news, felt his decades-long grudge vindicated. His memories of his own encounters with radicals in the SDS were enough to convince him of the desperate measures some might be willing to undertake. The taking over of administration buildings. The short-sighted demands including curricular changes and tenure decisions. The FBI agent went on to confirm his worst fears. THE GSLF was believed to be responsible for a similar crime at SUNY Stony Brook. In addition, the group had also placed several bomb threats in the past year, one of which shut down the main branch of the New York Public Library for an entire afternoon. Willingham had heard a story about the GSLF on NPR, too, that suggested Bureau agents were tired of being shown up by the Front, wanted desperately to bust up this group who had made them look like amateurs in the media. These curious developments had led Willingham to suspect that The Nonsense Shadow might very well be an impostor.

"If in fact this turns out to be the case, Mr. Sweeney—if in fact The Nonsense Shadow turns out to be nothing more than a fabulist, a deluded megalomaniac acting on his own—then we need a plan to smoke him out, to expose this terrorist as the poseur he is."

Sweeney nodded his head with cautious approval, willing to hear out this peculiar man whose passion for art was beginning to impress him as much as his love for the track. He prepared himself for another dramatic digression when he thought he heard, in an adjacent room, the muted sound of a cat landing on hardwood, then scampering away into silence. And as if on cue from the cat, Willingham, so pleased with the plan he was about to unfold that he could barely contain himself, began. "Mr. Sweeney, I want you to place another ad in the Sunday *Times* requesting that The Nonsense Shadow mail to me a typed copy of the *Requiem's* final page for verification of authenticity. I believe that I, of all the James scholars alive, I alone am uniquely fitted to judge whether or not a story was penned by the Master's hand. If the story meets certain specifications, bears the unmistakable imprint of the Master's genius, then I will pay the entire sum. In a single drop. Include in the ad that I will allow The Nonsense Shadow two weeks to respond. Let our friend understand that it is now I who am in the driver's seat. Are we understood?"

With no protest this time, Sweeney agreed to do as he was told. He realized by now that such protests were futile with a man like Willingham. In addition, Willingham, who had now taken out a tin of Dunhill *Royal Yacht* Tobacco and was packing a meerschaum he'd produced from his blazer, insisted that Sweeney wait to be contacted and make no attempt to call his apartment in the coming weeks. He had reason to believe, he said—lighting his pipe as a gleam shown in his eye—that the FBI might soon have him under surveillance. While ushering Sweeney to the front door, he made one final request.

"I expect we won't hear from our colleague for some time," he said, releasing the deadbolt but not opening the door. "At any rate, I would prefer that you not leave the city or take any sort of extended vacation that might remove you for more than a three hours' drive from my apartment. The Nonsense Shadow could reply at any minute, and he could be dangerous, as cornered beasts tend to be. I might require your expertise in self-defense. In any case, I myself have purchased a handgun as a precautionary measure."

Sweeney, fearing Willingham was getting carried away with a sense of intrigue, nonetheless assured him that he would do as told, for he had at least one other project that, it had recently been brought to his attention, would require his concentration in the coming weeks.

SIX DAYS LATER, WHILE ON the bus out to the Meadowlands, Sweeney's beeper unexpectedly went off. He placed a call from the track to Willingham, who sounded distressed and asked Sweeney to meet him at his apartment at eleven o'clock that night. Sweeney, seeing no other course of action possible, agreed to do so.

He arrived to find Willingham exhausted, uncharacteristically disheveled—ascot askew—and the smell of alcohol heavy on his breath. The distraught scholar ushered Sweeney once again into his study, offered his charge a drink—which Sweeney declined, having had several at the track that afternoon—then sat down behind his desk in his now familiar roost. Six stacks of twenties, placed in perfect rows, sat on the left side of the desk next to a tin of Dunhill, and a handgun lay to the right. Directly before Willingham lay an opened envelope. He removed its contents and read silently, nodding his head with apparent pleasure as he did so. Sweeney remained quiet. A good half minute passed before Willingham spoke.

"My dear, loyal Sweeney, you cannot imagine the great pleasure this letter has given me. The relief, the satisfaction of having one's wildest dreams realized. For you see, I hold in my hands a copy of the final page of the Master's *Requiem*. Let me take the opportunity right now to tell you that its brilliance exceeds even my high expectations. I'd been prepared to pay for the entire manuscript but realize now that is not required. The story has…necessitated a different course of action."

He stared vacantly at the desk before him, licked his lips, smiled silently for a few seconds, and then continued. "It is as if the Master had read my mind before I'd been born, as if he'd looked into my eyes and laid bare my deepest desires, whispered into my ear my secret name. This letter confirms a longing I've had since I first read a story by my beloved James. For you see, the Master's final tale…is mine."

"From this single page I can glean the entire *Requiem* itself, and what a masterpiece it must be! Only James could have produced such a work. A plot worthy of 'The Beast in the Jungle,' a protagonist every bit the equal of John Marcher or Spencer Brydon. Oh, glorious work of my Master's hands. So fearfully, so wonderfully made! You see, Sweeney, the *Requiem* is my story, the story of a brilliant, unappreciated scholar who seeks, in his retirement, to track down the lost manuscript of his deceased paragon, a manuscript referenced in letters and diaries, but somehow mysteriously vanished. He finds the story after years of digging through archives, toiling in the thankless work of the scholar, only to discover that the story – and here is the genius of James – the story's plot is virtually identical to the chronicle of his own search for the lost manuscript. The protagonist finds that his hero had invented his quest before he himself had undertaken it. Before he himself was, a tale had prophesied his existence! Before he himself was, the Master had made him so. Spoken him into being. Written him… into *existence*. Ah, Sweeney, can you not see? The *Requiem* has crowned my life's efforts, for it confirms what I had always wished for, and long suspected, but been too modest to admit. I have no need for the actual manuscript of the *Requiem* now, nor for anything else. These words are my fulfillment. This, Sweeney, is justice. To know that, in the end, I am worthy of my Master's pen—thank God—that is enough."

Sweeney was disturbed by the unexpected climax toward which the previous months of work seemed to be moving. But Willingham continued, undeterred. "And as this was how the *Requiem's* plot came to an end, so this is how mine shall, too..." But at the very moment Willingham had finished his riddling statement, Sweeney's attention was distracted by the sound of a cat that seemed to have landed atop one of the bookshelves in the study. Sweeping his eyes quickly about the room, he saw nothing. And then returning them to his employer, he saw it was too late. He could not redirect the moment before him through another door. The gun had already been raised, but incredibly, Willingham's heart raced ahead of his hand, granting him in death what he'd always longed for in life: a delicious and unexpected twist of plot. Even before the trigger could be pulled, his body had collapsed, his life extinguished the instant his enormous head had hit the desktop with an unsettling and dull thump.

A half minute passed. Reaching across the desk, Sweeney felt for a pulse along the crimsoned collar-line of his slumping interrogator, noting the look of carnal expectation still drawn upon the face. Then he bit down on his lower lip and began to tap his fingers upon the desk, wondering if he had chosen the right line of work. Or at least the right client to work for. So much seemed lost on this lonely, desperate figure. A minute passed. The ticking of a clock from somewhere in the apartment became audible. Finally, Sweeney let out a sigh, picked a ball of wax from his ear, flicked it across the study, and checked his watch. He stood up, walked around the desk, leaned over Willingham, and taking a pocket square out of his coat, carefully dislodged the gun from his employer's grasp, and placed it in a desk drawer. Then he removed the final page of The Requiem, still improbably clutched in the other hand. He stared at the single sheet of paper, rolled it into a cone and held it aloft in his left hand, like a taper, and then taking a lighter from the coat pocket where he always kept a pack of Camel No Filters, lit it. The sheet hissed into flame, burning with a luminescent quality that glowed especially bright in the presence of the study's dark woods and burgundy upholsteries. When the consummation was nearly complete, he dropped the remainder into an ashtray beside the stacked bills, and watched it curl and char. He lingered a few moments to consider the mysterious power of pen and paper. *Dangerous things, words*, he recalled. And he smiled.

Then The Nonsense Shadow wiped the ash from his fingertips,

pocketed the stacks of bills and the tin of Dunhill, and silently left the apartment.

ON THE BACK PAGE OF the Metro Section of the next edition of the Sunday *Times*—beneath an article about the still unsolved suicide of a retired, Yale English professor—appeared a small story of little general interest. On the previous Friday, police and FBI agents, acting on a tip from an anonymous source, had raided the Yonkers apartment of three Columbia graduate students who had taken summer internships at Yale's prestigious Beinecke Library. Two of the students were from Tarrytown and one from Scarsdale, and each had managed to work his way into debt from school and, apparently, a nasty gambling habit nurtured in the many underground poker parlors of Manhattan and frequent trips to Foxwoods and the Meadowlands. Agents found a manifesto penned by the GSLF demanding, among other conditions, a universal tuition waiver and comprehensive dental care for all Teacher Assistants. The joint operation conducted with the New York City police had also led to the discovery of a trunk full of stolen maps and manuscripts, most likely cut out from the Beinecke's rare book collection with an exacto knife, a cachet both agents and officers believed was being unloaded on the black market for cash. Toward the end of the article, Police Spokesman Brian Stevens was quoted as identifying several of the more prominent stolen items: a dozen maps from the first published accounts of Hudson's and Cook's expeditions, a rare color woodcut from a seventeenth century English Bible, a first edition small book printing of Lewis Carroll's "The Hunting of the Snark," and a faded carbon of a Henry James short story whose disappearance had of late caused a minor stir in select academic circles.

But Sweeney had noticed none of this. He had no time for such indulgence. In fact, he'd barely had time to hastily sketch the first draft of *The Requiem* on the back pages of a program between races the previous week at the Meadowlands. The final version he'd just finished on the bus in traffic on the way home that same night. And even on this day, hardly a week later, he'd only had time to skim the sports page – O'Neil singled in Henderson for an extra-inning Yankee victory – and make a mental note of the following day's racing times. The rest of the paper, Metro section included, Sweeney broke down and unfolded. He wrapped these large square sheets about his dishes, which he then packed into an old cardboard banker's box that sat next to another equally old box labeled H. James Collection. Yesterday, after two days of searching, he'd found a nice apartment on the Upper West Side, one that he could finally now afford. One that would make him a neighbor of sorts, with his former employer. And one that was large enough to accommodate the cat which had recently come into his possession. A cat he named Nilly.

All told, he was pleased with his good fortune, but a little disappointed in himself, for he'd eaten again at Rocco's. The diner was four blocks south of his new apartment, and he figured that maybe—since Harrigan was a decent guy and had given a good tip on the Belmont—he'd give him a chance to redeem himself. Harrigan proved unworthy of the gesture, though. The gas lodged in Sweeney's intestines seared his sides, bubbled out every so often only to retreat into the dark recesses of his bowels, as quickly as it had shot forth. The pain was crippling, and after he'd mailed a large check to Yale's Urban Improvement Corps, he had lost a good portion of the morning curled up in bed.

Despite this pain, he now managed to corral the chaos of his apartment into an orderly row of boxes. He suspected it wouldn't last long, though, that soon enough his new place would become, despite his best intentions, just as messy as his old place. Yet he didn't find the thought demoralizing. In fact, he didn't even find the thought, being too busy for such speculation. In a flash of insight, though, it had occurred to him he was doing "pretty good" – better than some others, anyhow. For the time being he had been allowed the means to get by all right. Instinct suggested to him that he could make it last longer than most. That he was on a run, of sorts. And he felt lucky. Indeed, it was part of Sweeney's nature not to let any circumstances flatter him, just as it was part of his nature not to let anything fluster him, either. He understood his limits. Life was a riddle, he knew, that resisted both reason and emotion. Upon its mysteries, he would neither despair nor presume. And though not without hope, Sweeney had long suspected that, in the final account, it was not only nonsense that would weigh in most heavily, but that it was, always already—and in spite of the best made plans—just nonsense.

Scenes from an Unfinished Church

THE APE HAD FOUND HIM out, and this he could not bear. He felt naked. Violated. Morally dressed down by a beast. It was absurd, for only the most freakish of circumstances had even brought him to the crowded church service, where he'd found himself lost in thought rather than impressed by the pageantry. Not a man given to theological speculation, he was nonetheless struck by the thought: Could a beast be blessed?

Decidedly not, he concluded, yet when he had looked back up at the procession of animals making their way down the nave, escorted by parishioners, he found the ape staring directly at him—nodding, grinning. The chimp had eyed him as if an equal, and this he resented. It was as if the beast had heard his thoughts or sensed his false communion, yet insisted on communicating: "Kinsman! Brother!" His face must have betrayed his contempt, for the ape began to howl and yip, hoot and gnash. And then finally, laugh. He recoiled. Chaos ensued.

All he could remember after that was he had screamed and turned violently away from the animals and bumped into an old man, knocking him to the floor of the cathedral. All hell then broke loose. The elephant struck first, shattering chairs and trampling dozens in its confusion, and then a pack of dogs fell upon the priest and a llama kicked its way through the crowd, and while a falcon toppled tapers before wheeling its way through the dark vaulted heights, five thousand souls collapsed in fear or rushed to the exits. St. Francis would not have been pleased. These beasts would not be blessed.

He had escaped the cathedral and run to the safety of the park, where few dared venture after dark. He roamed the park's paths and meadows the entire night, smiting stones with a makeshift staff, howling, cursing, waking dreamers from Harlem to Midtown. Even the crack dealers and whores steered clear, for they did not recognize the look in his eye. At dawn he found himself beneath the statue of Alice, at the right hand of nonsense. He'd always been drawn to this monument to the Oxford mathematician, so out of place in this new world. As out of place as he himself. And though he was quite certain that few could have possibly witnessed his fall, he would not be consoled. So he thought to himself: after such humiliation, such shame, why not kill?

Beyond Alice's shoulder, some thirty blocks to the northwest, he thought he could just make out the archangel, high atop the cathedral. Mocking him. Trumpeting forth his folly. Not an hour later he was in his Wall Street office, sipping coffee and reading snatches of The Times' account of the previous evening's chaotic church service while charting the overnight movement in the Asian market.

~~~~~

FATHER TIMOTHY WAS VEXED. He had slept none that night, running over the scene again and again in his mind. Revising his actions, recrafting his account for Captain O'Neil. He expected to have to answer more questioning from the police this morning. It was not every day that a riot broke out in the largest Gothic church in the world. For over ten years, he had participated in the Blessing of the Animals, and each time the feast day had gone off without a hitch. He could not understand what had happened, and deep inside he feared it was a sign. On a more conscious level, he dreaded the significance of it that he knew the ranters and millenarian activists would no doubt make.

For it was a city of prophets, and though early in his career he had relished the part of his office that require he dismantle, expose, and condemn such figures, he had of late grown wary of this duty. He had begun to suspect they knew something he did not. The wariness that accompanied this thought hounded him night and day. Even while negotiating the busy streets of Morningside Heights, as he found himself doing this morning on the way to work, he could not escape the vision of this mob of mad prophets. It would not let him be.

He had to remind himself again and again that his plight was no different from those of earlier generations. And the truth was, he fancied, that by moonlight, there was probably little to distinguish this

neighborhood and its cathedral of the twentieth century from its coun-
terparts of the twelfth. Save a few streetlamps and city noises, Father
Timothy liked to think that even a sensibility as discerning as Aqui-
nas' would have had a difficult time distinguishing St. John the Divine
from Chartres. To a simple peasant of that earlier century, he imagined
they'd be as one; the passage of time would not exist until dawn. Try
though he might, he could never quite convince himself of this.

And yet if his sympathies were exaggerated, he felt certain that
even the most skeptical would allow a certain romance to the Manhattan moonlight. It could be democratic and leveling in a way that
the harsh light of day could not be. Yet when it was all said and done,
he had never been able to fully accept the idea of the equality of the
human experience, in part because he could not bear the thought that
a man like this one now approaching him could be his true equal. He
crossed the street as if to get some coffee and avoid his congregant,
but the old man did the same. He caught up to Father Timothy as the
latter had just given a street vendor a handful of change for a cup of
coffee.

"Don't think it's no sign, Father."

"Willie!" Father Timothy exclaimed, with feigned surprise, as he
turned to greet him, spilling some of the contents of his cup onto
his hand and barely stifling an oath in the process. "Good morning. I
didn't see you coming."

"It's a sign, Father. I know you don't like such talk, but it's a sign."

"Willie, I'm not sure," he began, but Willie continued undeterred.

"I've seen them for months out now. Seen them coming. The signs
are real. And they're all around us. And this one, this is one has me
worried."

Father Timothy wiped his hand clean on the sleeve of his overcoat,
stalling a few seconds in a desperate attempt to search his mind for a
response, before trying politely to cut off his interlocuter.

"Willie, my good friend, what happened last night was a terrible
tragedy, and we must pray for the rebuilding of the church and the
repose of those souls now departed—as well as for the full recovery
of those injured—but I am not sure if we should call it a *sign*. Not a
sign in the way you mean. No, this was no sign Willie, but a terrifying
and unfortunate," and here he struggled for the right word, "mishap."

But his aged congregant would have none of it.

"And I saw the chimp, too. Saw the chimp that started it all. That done it. Heard him all last night. And saw him on the tower not three hours ago. Before dawn."

This disturbed Father Timothy. He had been assured by the police and animal control that all the animals that had participated in the ceremony of the previous evening had been captured and were scheduled to be either returned to their owners or, if necessary, put under that afternoon. All the animals had been accounted for. All, that is, except the chimp. But the police had promised him that this would be kept confidential in the interest of preserving calm within the neighborhood that had already suffered so much confusion. In fact, several teams from animal control and the Central Park Zoo were still discreetly scouring the cathedral complex in search of the chimp and would be until it was caught.

"Nonsense, my good Willie. Captain O'Neil assured me last night that all the animals had been rounded up. Perhaps you saw another one of those strays that's been gorging on the trash outside the refectory. I saw one just the other day, and its size astonished me. Or maybe it was one of the little choir boys playing another prank. At a distance, and at our age," he intoned sympathetically, though Willie was twice as hold as he, "men are given to seeing things."

"A cat don't walk upright. And a little boy don't climb hundred foot towers," Willie said, gesturing at the cathedral across the street behind him.

"Three hundred feet, Willie. Which makes your claim all the more...I'm sure it was early—not yet sunup, you say?—and I'm sure you saw something that looked like a chimp. But it wasn't. There is no chimp, Willie. All the beasts have been driven from the church."

"And I saw that man, too. He was there last night. The one from class."

Father Timothy momentarily froze. He knew exactly whom Willie was talking about, for they'd discussed this topic two months earlier. The man was a student in one of the cathedral's continuing education classes created both for outreach and as a sort of public relations and marketing ploy to inform curious, and hopefully wealthy, neighbors of the cathedral's projects and aspirations. It had taken him weeks

to ease Willie's mind about this man, who'd stopped frequenting the
church and its classes as quickly and mysteriously as he'd begun his
visits, and so who by this definition was hardly peculiar as this practice was more common than not among neighbors. The city was filled
with dilletantes who passed from one fancy to another.

"Speaking of your classes, Willie, how have they been going? I
was hearing great things about your work from Mr. Picard before
he had to return to Marseilles. He bragged about you constantly and
said you were his top apprentice. Mr. Verity agreed. Said that if you'd
been born a thousand years ago in Paris, you'd surely have made
master mason."

Father Timothy had helped revive this neighborhood program
to which he alluded, whereby the local unemployed might be taught
a skill and use it to earn a modest living while helping complete the
church, and it was under the aegis of this program that Willie had
been leading guided tours of the cathedral, working on statuary, and
even helping teach the sculpture portion of one of the continuing ed
classes. But attendance had dropped precipitously between sessions
two and three, and though a few donations of considerable size had
kept the program from oblivion, Father Timothy suspected its days
were numbered. It was only when attendance had dwindled from the
original twenty-three to five that one particular student become dis-
tinguishable, and this only because he stood half a foot taller than
the rest. And never said a word. He arrived early, listening with great
intensity and taking extensive notes on the lectures about medieval
practice and artistic technique. And then late last summer during a
class, when implements were circulated among the students as part
of a lesson plan, he lingered over the chisel and mallet, lost in contemplation of them and not passing them along until Picard had twice
reminded him to do so. After the most recent lecture, Willie was
certain this man had hidden a tooth chisel in his overcoat because
he noticed one was missing when he was cleaning up the classroom
afterward. He showed Picard the empty slot in the foam encased
valise: eleven implements fit snugly into their assigned slots, but one
was clearly absent. He'd even asked Father Timothy to have security
detain the man after class; Picard seemed to approve of the request.
But Timothy had stalled, suspecting that the man's bespoke attire,

and especially his shoes, might suggest he was responsible for one of the large checks the program had generated. Instinctively, he assumed that the chisel had surely been misplaced, figuring it was worth neither the risk of embarrassment nor lost donations to accuse a man of something so trivial when he was coming into support a church program after a long day at the office. Willie had not been satisfied with his actions that night after class, and Father Timothy suspected he would not be satisfied now, either.

Still, he thought the subtle change in conversation deft on his part, and he anticipated some relief from steering Willie away from his obsession with signs and mysterious men and onto a topic that would flatter the old man and obligate him to abandon his troubling line of inquiry. Father Timothy thought wrongly.

"That chimp saw something in that man. Something terrible. Same thing I saw from him in class."

"Yes, well your class can be accused of doing nothing except brilliant work. I do hope you'll resume it in the spring," he added, though he knew that recent meetings of the Trustees had deemed that highly unlikely.

"He's who were looking for. Find that man, and he'll have some answers. Bring him in and let the cops question him."

Father Timothy was at a loss. He tried to recall that first conversation about signs that they'd had months earlier, searching his mind to remember what he'd said that allowed him to allay Willie's unreasonable fears and dispatch him with all due speed. His memory was a bit fuzzy on details. Indeed, recently he'd become half aware that much of what he said at such unexpected moments was inconsistent, a mere attempt to keep his head above water and not appear incompetent in the presence of a parishioner. Though he knew no one was a monolith, he also knew some degree of consistency was a must. He wondered could he regurgitate that sermon now to rid himself of Willie, and he set about trying simultaneously to appraise the long-term memory of his congregant and recall the sermon to his own mind. Then, he had appealed to Willie's sense of community and inclusiveness, insisting on the church's mission of being a sanctuary, albeit an imperfect one, to all.

"Don't you see Willie," he recalled he had said, "even a flawed order is better than none at all. No church, no real clergy, would claim to be morally superior to any other person or community. That's a heresy, one the church itself condemned a thousand years ago. What distinguishes the church is its understanding of God, of human nature and redemption, its description of sin and evil and the proper way to atone for them. The church is not necessarily better than any other community. But, and this is important, Willie—the church acknowledges its trespasses and *will* submit to authority. Authority outside itself. The authority of God. It must. And that's the sign of its legitimacy. It will confess and submit, and in its submission, lies the hope for its salvation. And for *all* of our salvation."

Willie had seemed impressed at the time, though Father Timothy suspected Willie wondered whether or not he himself believed those words. Regardless, Willie had left his office soon afterwards. At the present moment, Father Timothy realized he would have to labor forth with another such performance to again be rid of his inquisitor, raising his game as the stakes themselves had been elevated. As a younger clergyman, he had actually relished such chances to perform, but he had to admit he frequently felt imperiled at loving his delivery of the message more than the words themselves. He had to check this tendency while revisiting this sermon in his mind. Eventually, he decided upon a variation of that earlier theme.

"Willie, let this man be, for heaven's sake. We must remember, before we rush to judgment, that just as the church is incomplete, so, too, is man. You can't prosecute a man because you didn't like his look. Because he didn't conform to your sense of order. Because you found him disagreeable." And then, trying to bring the conversation onto ground that would disarm Willie, he concluded paternally, "We must be tolerant of differences. We must celebrate our diversity. We must agree," and here he paused dramatically before dropping the keystone into place, "to disagree."

Father Timothy was pleased with this performance, but again Willie was not.

"Disagree? But it's a *sign*, Father. You don't disagree with a sign. It's not ours to choose to agree or disagree. There is no disagree. It's war, Father. Not disagreement. That why Michael got himself a sword, isn't it," and he nodded over across Amsterdam toward the statue of the Archangel in the cathedral Close, just visible from curbside.

"Sword or no sword, Willie. All are welcome."

"Father, it's a *sign*, I know it is. I've had dreams."

"Trust me, Willie, there is no sign. There are no signs. No dreams."

Willie remained upset.

"I know what I saw. That chimp was climbing the tower. And that man doesn't know order. He's outside your order. Your words… they don't describe him. He has no order."

"Mystery men. Chimps climbing towers. New York under attack—you've seen King Kong too many times, Willie. Now go home and get some rest and try to forget the night's events."

"I know what I saw!"

Father Timothy disregarded these comments and looked down at his watch, "My goodness—it's almost eight o'clock, Willie. I'd better get going."

Father Timothy had been defeated, and he knew it. So he finished his coffee and started a casual trot across the street, eyeing the traffic so as to excuse his silence at Willie's remark.

"He was outside your office window, too. Howling and scratching." Father Timothy tried to act as if he hadn't heard this last part, tried to act as if all his concentration had been focused on avoiding the early morning traffic along Amsterdam as he crossed toward the cathedral.

"You wait, Father. You'll see him. But Willie'll protect you good people. I know the signs."

"Willie, take care of yourself and don't be a stranger. Come see me sometime," Father Timothy shouted as he leapt upon the opposite curb and looked back, relieved now at the safe distance between him and his inquisitor. "Miss Thompson's birthday is on Wednesday, and we'll have some cake in the office for sure. Stop by. I'll save you a big piece. They're always asking about you, you know. She's quite fond of you. At any rate, Willie, don't be a stranger. I must go now—onward, Willie, onward!"

And with that, he turned and headed toward his office within the church compound, a half dozen buildings on eleven acres in Harlem.

He felt confused, resentful, and more than a bit curious as to how Willie knew about the chimp. He should not have that knowledge, and Father Timothy planned to give the police station a call as soon as he got to his office. Word had somehow leaked, and they could not afford this. They could not allow for certain elements within the neighborhood to stir up emotions and fears at a time like this. The beast had to be caught, and it had to be done with proper discretion and tact.

He thought back over the scene. It had been a menagerie run amok. He had been there, but when the chaos began he dashed immediately for the Founder's Tomb directly behind the high altar, where he huddled behind the iron grille until the confusion subsided. He had to confess that it had struck him as more than just a random and unfortunate occurrence. This was not merely the unruly behavior of brutes. But could it be a *sign*?

The amount of damage done to the cathedral was astonishing, seemed excessive and disproportionately thorough to the amount of time—surely no more than five minutes—that chaos reigned in the great and unfinished church. The congregation had scattered amid a confusion of tongues and profanities. Toppled tapers burst into new life as they consumed banners and tapestries. Tongues of flame raced around the apse, forming a fiery scrim before which the animals' rebellion played out. Had the floor not been flagstone and the ceiling not some hundred and fifty feet high, smoke would have claimed many, for each flame seemed to hatch a hundred hooded minions that ate up the church's inside.

Fortunately, the proper attendants from the fire department, animal control, and the zoo were all on hand. But it was as if the beasts understood the significance of the interior and wasted no time or effort on the trivial. The giraffe had wandered confused in the apse, launching tables of tapers and butting windows, destroying one, before eventually getting routed from the chapel of St. Columba and out into the Close before capture. Countless chairs had been overturned and destroyed. The donkey had chased down the crucifer and harassed an altar boy into a state of shock. Two pigs had smashed a bulletin board, while an armadillo singlehandedly ate or tore apart a few dozen hymnals. The dogs snatched at stoles and vestments but had quickly been scattered out into the night. The llama, no doubt terrified at the ruckus, chewed up a few tapestries before managing to get its head stuck inside a crypt of the columbarium. When finally pulled free, it was covered in ash.

As one would expect, the elephant had done the most damage, scattering the choir, destroying the friendship menorah and pulpit, then overturning the high altar, trampling eight congregants—two of whom died of heart attacks—and eventually running the length of the crowded nave before bursting out onto Amsterdam. Police and a zookeeper finally shot it dead in the middle of the street not thirty yards from the gates to Columbia. All the animals, save the neighborhood dogs and cats whose masters had brought them to be blessed, had been accounted for and were, sadly, scheduled to be destroyed that afternoon. All except the ape.

During the questioning of witnesses, a janitor reported to police that she had seen a chimp above the fray, swooping from a chandelier with a taper stand in one hand, scaling tracery from the great rose to the lesser before disappearing into the smokey and vaulted heights. She was sworn to secrecy by the investigating officer, because the police and church staff realized the danger such an account might create. Urban dwellers, and their overactive imaginations, hunger for signs, for some sort of meaning beyond the horizon circumscribed by skyscrapers, ticker tape, and the hours of the workday.

And the truth was that what frightened Father Timothy the most was that, in his deepest heart of hearts, it had struck him as a sign, too. He could not confess this to Willie. Or to anyone else. But this is what had kept him up all night, and this of all things was not what he wanted. Since childhood he'd dreaded he wouldn't be able to make it through life without committing some terrible crime. But so far he had. All through seminary he had prayed to be through with life without having to confront any signs. And again, thus far his prayers had been answered. He didn't think he possessed the mettle to deal with such matters. But last night had changed the trajectory of everything. He thought he deserved better than this.

For he daily engaged in an honest appraisal of his strengths and weaknesses. He felt quite certain he was a hard worker. Responsible husband. Good with kids. A devoted volunteer. Good Sunday school teacher. Very good sermons—occasionally, perhaps, even great. Less learned than most supposed, yet excellent at disguising this. Plagued with doubts. Vain. Full of lust. Resentful. Lately dogged by racist thoughts. Victimless crimes all, but wrong nonetheless. Yet what most terrified him was the thought of having his faith put to the test. For who, he would always wonder to himself, pronounced when a test had arrived? He thought he might pass if someone or something would only distinguish the tests from the trivial. Would announce such trials beforehand.

And so he remained uncertain if indeed the animals had renounced their brotherhood with man, rejecting the church's holy rights and man's smug sense of self and purpose. Father Timothy knew that though the destruction of the church had been animal in act, it might be cosmic in significance. Was it, he dreaded, an act foretold by Revelation, carried out by dumb prophets of the apocalypse? A promise of a dark millennium? He loved the church dearly, so grand in conception if flawed in execution. And he loved St. John's: "God's footstool," he fondly called it. Here, man had striven to build a New Jerusalem, a St. John's upon a hill in Harlem, yet the verdict from last night seemed to be clear. Man's vision and piety had been found wanting.

These beastly lords of misrule mocked man's claim of dominion and the attendant presumptuousness required to claim to have built a house of God. And so in the nave of this largest church in the capital city of the world, the animal kingdom recoiled from man's hypocrisy, severing ties once and for all. Though brutes without language, they knew man well enough and recognized the cathedral for what Father Timothy sometimes feared it to be: a Tower of Babel, a god of the belly.

~~~~~

AT THE PRECISE TIME WILLIE was detaining Father Timothy on the street in Harlem, a figure in an office across town had lost, won, then lost again, over twenty million dollars.

"What's on tap tonight, Lace?" a nervous voice asked, startling the tall, broad figure at a window desk whose attention moved from computer screen to a copy of The Times that lay spread out before him. The short and lumpy graduate of Adelphi relished using his co-worker's nickname in public, for it made him feel initiated. His co-worker merely tolerated the annoyance.

Knowledge of William Burnside Lynch III's nickname flourished because of a story that had migrated with him from his Amherst fraternity, through the Harvard MBA program and into the board-rooms at Morgan Stanley, a story that he'd done nothing to dispel or embroider and that recounted how after one night of especially depraved debauchery during his freshman year he'd ended up in the town detox cell where, for his own safety, procedure require he be di-vested of his valuables, his belt, and his shoelaces and made to spend the night. Upon his release the next morning, a policeman informed him that his shoelaces had been misplaced, and he flew into such a rage demanding he be reimbursed, actually taking a swing at the cop, that his fraternity brothers had to drag him away from the sta-tion before he got into more trouble. From that March day forward, he'd been known as "Shoelace," or "Lace" for short. Classmates and coaches forgot his real name, and even his sisters took to calling him it in moments of frustration.

"Gonna go boozing tonight, Lace, huh?" his colleague asked, try-ing to pry some form of recognition out of his coworker.

"Nope."

"No? 'Cause, well, me and some guys, we were thinking we might go boozing. Want to catchup with us late night?"

Lace shook his head from side to side.

"You going to the Knicks' game then, I bet? I'd forgotten they were back in town."

No answer.

"You're on the prowl, then, aren't you? Fucking animal, Lace!"

Again, he received no reply.

"I bet you got a case of the yellow fever, don't you. You're a beast, Lace, you know that?"

He just shook his head from side to side, bored.

"Animal. Don't you ever rest?"

"You can rest when you die."

"Oh, that's good."

"Good."

"What, did the yen gain overnight?"

"Yup."

"You lose a little money already, Lace?"

"Yup."

"Your little geisha girl gonna be upset with you—she still gonna take care of you, Lace?"

"They all take care of me."

"Where's she at, Lace, down near The Garden? Tommy goes down there all the time. Caught some shit, though. A strain that wouldn't die."

"Good for Tommy."

"You find her on Channel 35, Lace, or in the yellow pages?"

"Clever."

"She must be good, looks like you got a new suit for her. Cheo?" He nodded.

"And you're wearing your Lobb's too, I see."

"A man needs his shoes."

"Yes he does."

"To kick that ass."

"You're a cold blooded son of a bitch, Lace."

"Go fuck yourself now. I need to make some money."

"Get your roll on, Lace. We'll be at O'Malley's late night, if you're interested. You know where that is?"

He received no response.

"All right, man. Hope to see you there. O'Malley's around 11:00. You're my dawg, Lace. You the man."

Oblivious to this invitation, he continued reading *The Times* article, thinking he might take lunch in the Park if it wasn't too cold.

~~~~~

WILLIE HAD BECOME WORRIED. Worried that where he saw a workshop others saw a museum. Worried he had been reduced to a tour guide at a theme park. Worried that Father Timothy had not taken his words seriously enough. Worried that Father Timothy had not taken his own words seriously enough. And even worried that he himself might have overreacted. He was happy he had a job—he'd gone years without a steady one—but he didn't like the idea that the church was becoming its own industry. Was consumed with the idea of revenue streams. He liked giving tours, and he enjoyed helping teach the introduction to sculpture class well enough, though he knew that without Mr. Picard's help the classes probably would not resume in the spring. This uneasiness was compounded by the fear that the church had become so desperate for funds that it was whoring its soul. And Willie was frightened that he had become part of the problem: giving tours to kodak-snapping tourists and teaching a class to anxiety-ridden brokers seeking to ease their nerves and have something at their fingertips more substantial, meaningful, and enduring than a palm pilot full of stock quotes.

For throughout the summer on every Tuesday and Thursday nights, from six to until seven thirty—the brokers wanted to be gone before darkness fell in Harlem—some twenty well-dressed students made their awkward way into the cathedral grounds, "Not for mass," as Willie was fond of saying, "but for class." Willie worried that more than a few of them didn't study their craft to bring glory to God or celebrate creation, but to ease their own nerves so they could return to work and log more fifteen-hour days. If they could pick up some new subject matter for cocktail parties, be part of an unusual trend, then all the better. Initially, this did not worry Willie too much. But it had soon started to bother him deeply. The therapeutic quality of working with clay was not lost on Willie, still it seemed a bit hopeless; after thirty minutes of art history slides and an hour of trying to mold the ineffable—a cherubim, the ark, the paraclete—they flattened out their clay into a cake, returned it to a tray which Willie re-shelved like a mortician. How much good the class did for its students or the church was debatable; the tuition was fairly high given the cost of materials, and though the students might buy a t-shirt or a few books from the cathedral gift shop, in a month or two most would have moved on to the next trend: Pilates, Fung Schuea, Lincoln on the Stock Market, Lao Tzu on relationships. It was an unholy economy. And for too long Willie had paid rent from it. But there had been at least two large donations that seemed to have come from one of the students. Donations large enough to pay a few months' utilities, Father Timothy had told him, though he would not mention specific figures. More than once, Willie had run some projections through his head. He knew they were rudimentary, at best, but any way he cut it, the number at which he arrived was enormous.

Three hours had passed since his conversation with Father Timothy, and he hadn't gotten much done: visited with some vendors, bought a newspaper, fed some pigeons. He wouldn't be giving any tours today. He bought a sandwich and then went across Amsterdam, entered the cathedral Close, and sat on a bench in front of the statue of Michael. He loved the statue and the chain strand fence that surrounded it, where at intervals had been placed small sculptures crafted by children from the neighborhood and now immortalized next to plaques bearing their names. Father Timothy himself had been involved in this part of the project.

Father Timothy was a paradox, Willie thought. He liked him, flaky as he was. But he respected him more than liked him. No one put in more hours at the soup kitchen, planning the blood drive, working AIDS awareness week. He was a tireless volunteer. But he would not talk about church dogma. He avoided it. Didn't like conflict. And the church, Willie thought, was a strange place for a man who didn't like conflict. He stared blankly into the Peace Fountain.

Michael himself stood in the center of the fountain. Standing atop a double helix, he rose over thirty feet above the sidewalk, with a wingspan to match. With his sword extended downward, he pushed Lucifer into the chaos at his feet, where animals danced around him in celebration of his victory. Willie sat in the shadow of one of the great wings and wondered if Michael's vigil was still necessary. Was this warrior angel politically correct? Could he be softened? Made kinder, gentler? Had Michael secretly shrugged his shoulders years ago and renounced involvement with mankind. Walked away from his vigil for good, tired of man's faithlessness? Willie wondered, too, if man had a use for Michael. And what, for that matter, was man's use, period? A sparrow hopped up to his feet. Instinctively, Willie fed him a piece of bread, then lit himself a cigarette. He stared into the archangel's face. Then he tore off a larger chunk from his sandwich and fed it to the birds from his cap.

~~~~~

WEATHER PERMITTING, HE HAD THE same lunch every day. He left the office for an hour and a half, which was no big deal since he usually worked until ten. He never took a cab, always walked, buying a sandwich from a food truck along the way. Ate it on the same bench in the park, next to Alice and overlooking the pond. The young girl was surrounded by her own menagerie of animals and quirky characters. It was an absurd scene and subject for a statue. And that was partly why he felt drawn to it. The idea of a garden within a city amused him, too. The belief that one could circumscribe the wild disturbed him. And yet it was an idea as old as Nebuchadnezzar. He was certain, though, that those who thought you could subdue and cultivate nature were fated to find out you could not.

Lately, he'd grown convinced that Central Park was the world's first theme park. Six Flags, Knotts Farm, even Coney Island: they each derived from this grandmother of all kitsche with its vendors and its carousel, its barkers, zoo, and paddle boats. Its museums, skating rinks, and performers. New Yorkers flocked to the park as if they were pilgrims, seeking their authentic identity in yoga classes held on the great lawn or while hiking on any of the wooded paths through the park's eight hundred and forty acres. They all thought the next guy was the tourist, believed that they themselves felt something more pure, understood the park's significance more thoroughly. This behavior amused him. He knew they were all tourists. That everyone was a tourist. Himself included. Always and only. A mother-fucking tourist. The thought troubled him not in the least. And if, in a moment of weakness, he imagined himself going home to the park, he only went home hating it as do all prodigals.

For in spite of itself, the park remained a paradox—a big lie. When Olmstead first began cultivating this arcadian ground, slaves were being auctioned off two hundred miles to the south. The park had survived a civil war and two world wars, a depression, several moon landings, and countless recessions and world championships. And the conflict had not subsided. It spoke, Lynch thought, to something universal in man: his need to subdue nature; nature's need to resist. Today, drugs were bought and sold in broad daylight, the homeless hounded picnickers, gangs roamed the carefully planned esplanades, and sodomites sought out their kind in the shrubbery.

The truth was that man liked the idea of a little swatch of wild in the heart of the city. Liked trying to keep his dark side on a leash, let it loose to roam the park meadows before calling it home to safety. A grand idea, that one can visit and revisit such a place at one's leisure. But it just didn't work that way. Yet he doubted that it wasn't the fate of America to be reduced to such a landscape. Pave the whole continent, he mused, but a new beast would emerge, adopt to the concrete waste and perpetuate the bloodlust. Which is why he loved Alice's statue the most. It was the center of an absurd world. Mocked the logic of poseurs. Threw all off balance. For the park, the park was a trick—the trick of civilized man—a half-assed attempt to go native. But you can't go back. You can't domesticate the true wild. Gate it and assign visiting hours. It's all or nothing. And if it's all, the price is high: everything. *Everything.* He liked the word. He had a hunger for everything. Wanted to take everything. It would be everything.

So he would wander the park, site of mankind's oldest fantasy, its oldest lie, pinned to a page of earth beneath skyscrapers and towers. The oldest lie writ large. For all to see. There he sat and ate his lunch. In the presence of liars.

~~~~~

OUT OF FEAR OF RUNNING into more confused parishioners, Father Timothy decided to order lunch in. Once again he was feeling troubled by his job. Though not quite thirty-eight, he was already gray, and the athletic figure that had graced the squash courts of Choate and Brown was quickly turning soft. He was plagued with doubts: about his job, his future, even the church itself. None could deny the fantastic history behind St. John's. Indeed, he'd become a learned student of its history and a connoisseur of its quirks. Nor could any deny the tangible good the church did in the community.

But lately he had begun to doubt the direction of the church. It seemed unreal to him: a world's fair of barkers and booths, an Epcot with jeweled crosses. The cost of such adornment was staggering. But hadn't Christ upbraided those who told Mary not to anoint his feet? Hadn't God detailed the elaborate construction of the tabernacle to Moses? Daily, he catechized himself on this subject. The church consumed him. He feared it was a symptom of the age, an age of dilettantes and self-congratulators, of monuments and museums dedicated to vulgarians or victims and countless halls of fame and awards shows presented by laughable 'academies' from every field of endeavor known to man. For good or bad, the church embodied some of this age.

But he could not decide whether St. John's was a vibrant eclecticism or a vulgar collage of such an age. Symbols abounded, all of them riven from their original context. There in the nave was a stone slab on which the Magna Carta had been signed, a menorah next to the high altar, images of football players, and even a stained-glass window of Henry Adams. Of all figures to enshrine in an episcopal church, Adams seemed one of the least likely candidates. Only eleventh-hour objections had disqualified Pound from being inducted into the cathedral's Poet's Corner, itself an idea stolen Westminster. Had these symbols been drained of significance? Reduced to the stuff of marketing gimmicks, commodities so as to fetch a price on the market of cultural clout? He himself had helped organize some of the projects that leant themselves to such an interpretation. "Passion accessories," a seminary professor of his had called such marketing and merchandise, and he felt as if he were one of the centurions at the foot of the cross, dividing garments to be auctioned off on eBay. Timothy knew, as well, that the congregation had no greater critic of this activity than Willie.

And once again it had been Willie who had confounded him. Father Timothy considered his well-intentioned, septuagenarian antagonist. The truth was he loved Willie and admired certain aspects of his character. He'd read his job application and found his Personal Statement compelling, knew he'd landed at Inchon and helped seize Kimpo Airfield, then returned home and eventually attended Pace for a year and a half. Knew that "Willie" was actually "Willem." From the casual asides of colleagues and Willie's paper work, he'd pieced together something of a biography, knew it was likely that the blood of all Manhattan ran through his veins: Dutch and Delaware, English and African. Knew that he'd been married once. And lost a child at a young age. He both sympathized with and respected his friend. And yet unhesitatingly he thought himself superior to Willie, and this troubled him. Why? Was it education? Race? Age? Income? A combination of these things? He'd long suspected that perhaps a small part of it was such a combination, the type of petty prejudices and vanities to which all humans fall prey. But at its root he feared it was something else, for he thought himself better than all others he met, too. The feeling was programmed into his DNA. It was what made him human. An intense selfishness and vanity made him think thusly of his fellows, and he knew that this was why he above all men needed community—why he needed the fellowship and discipline of the church.

He went to his window and looked out onto the cathedral Close. From the very start, he had been fascinated with the statue of Michael. Partly because he had objected to it, indeed to the very idea that in the year 2000 the church would need or subscribe to a belief in a figure like this most troubling of the angels. Partly because he had been appointed to co-lead the fundraiser that had underwritten the statue. And it was a fine piece of art, he had to admit: epic in proportion, vigorous in energy.

The sun was setting now, casting a pinkish hue over the streets of New York. A beautiful gloaming. He looked from the sky back to the statue, the product of his finest, if most conflicted, hour on the capital campaign. He had shaken hands with the Archbishop of York at the statue's dedication, an event that commemorated the 200th year of the Diocese of New York. It had been a grand pageant, perhaps the most elaborate in the history of St. John's. Tom Wright had been there. Rowan Williams, too. He gazed from the impressive wingspan to the shock of hair upon the archangel's head, down his powerful torso to the blurry figure of Lucifer being cast into hell. And there, sitting on a bench at Michael's feet, humbly feeding the birds out of his Yankees' cap, was Willie.

~~~~~

NEITHER FRIENDS NOR FAMILY WOULD have imagined he'd end up on Wall Street. He'd never given anyone a reason to think so. But then again, though he'd double majored in English and classics, he was a man of few words. This and his considerable size distinguished him. More so than graduating summa cum laude or winning the Cabot Prize for best Latin translation. His honors thesis had been the pride of the department, but he'd eschewed grad school for the lure of the Street. He'd worked three years for Goldman, left the "tribe," as he called it, for a Harvard MBA, then returned to a house better suited to his genealogy. His resume was impressive, so packed with achievements that he'd had to leave off it that he'd coauthored a paper with a chemistry professor and twice been named an All-New-England defender. But of all his achievements what he remained most proud of was hooking up with the niece of the Treasury Secretary. Indeed, it had been no small feat, more difficult, he felt certain, than the Cabot Prize.

He'd had his eye on her since freshman orientation, when she'd repeatedly used the word "ergo" in actual conversation with him. While waiting in line to register for classes, she had announced, half to herself but loud enough for others to hear, "I placed out of freshman English, ergo I'll take the Shakespeare class and Bloomsbury." She'd turned around to be sure he'd heard, and then asked him what he'd be taking. He was polite with her, and they actually became casual friends. He found her kind and thoughtful. But all the while he wanted her to pay for her initial pretension. Three and a half years later, she did just that. His greatest college thrill came during the night of his conquest, on the weekend of Winter Carnival, when at the peak of her degradation he remembered her us of "ergo." He smiled darkly at the thought, running his fingers through her hair, considering the fragile nape of her bare neck.

He was not sentimental. In the office, on the street, at the club—he always went for the jugular. He remembered curves of throat not names, and he despised small talk. If he could have beaten and murdered night itself he would have done so. In a heartbeat. Repeatedly. Then there were the dark moods.

Such as this one tonight. He'd lost money today and somebody was going to pay. There were no hard feelings involved. It's just the way it was. He left the office at about nine thirty and caught a cab up to 110th.

~~~~~

WILLIE HAD GONE TO BED early, but he couldn't sleep. He felt bad, wondered if he had been disrespectful to Father Timothy. He hoped not. He worried he may have over-reacted to an event which he really couldn't recall that clearly. The cathedral had been packed the night of the service. Maybe the man who bumped into him was not the man from his class. Maybe Father Timothy knew best. Willie hoped to see him soon so that he might apologize. It was true, the city was full of unusual people, but that didn't make them bad. Or evil. He smiled at the thought. But he didn't fall asleep for another hour.

~~~~~

THE TRUTH OF THE MATTER was this customer worried them. Though they made their living off of pitiful, lonely men, this one was different. Well groomed. Well dressed. Very professional. He kept conversation to the bare minimum. Always asked for the same girl. Always stayed for several hours. Left a large tip.

He didn't have any bizarre fetishes. He didn't care for the candles, the incense, the music that other clients paid good money for. His only unusual request was that the windows be left open. They figured it was so air could circulate, not so that passersby in the street below could hear him at work. He struck them more like a young congressman or a novitiate, both of which they'd serviced before, but which was still a little unsettling to them. Not even hypocrites like to see hypocrisy at that high a level. He was tall, broad, and good looking. He always asked for Suzie, the slender, twenty-year-old whose parents had fled a civil war in a distant country. She appreciated his business and honored his request for privacy. On this particular night, he did not stray from his routine. He paid up front. Told her exactly what he wanted, wasting no words. While he undressed, she thought she saw him smile darkly as he caught sight of himself in one of the many mirrors situated around the room, but she wasn't sure. And then he went to work like a vulture on a carcass.

Three hours after he had arrived he was still at work when he experienced the strange sensation that he was being watched. He did not necessarily mind this, as he'd requested it once before, but this time something seemed wrong. He pushed Suzie aside and turned around to face the back of the room, where one of several full-length mirrors stood and where a window admitted the cool October air and the muted street noises from several stories below. There, in the corner of the dark room, stood the ape.

He leaned forward and squinted hard into the darkness. A gust shook the half-drawn curtain, admitting a poor quality of light that nonetheless seemed to flesh out the squat, hairy witness. He froze and, perhaps for only the second time in his life, was terrified. He didn't know how much time had elapsed when Suzie, who'd been confused by his behavior, finally tracked his gaze to the room's corner and let out a scream. In an instant he had turned and struck her across the face, then wheeled back around to the chimp, but he was not there. He ran to the window, stumbling on an object on the floor. There was no sight of the ape on the fire escape. Or in the street blow. He stooped to pick up the object, turning it around in his hand. By now Suzie had regained her senses and picked up her cell phone on the nightstand. Before she could finish dialing, a taper stand struck her on the right temple, caving in her skull.

~~~~~

FATHER TIMOTHY LITERALLY RAN INTO Willie two days after their awkward curbside meeting. Willie had been invited to watch the planting of a scion from the Glastonbury Thorn in the church cloister. He was excited and had talked about it constantly for the past day. The church gift store cashier and security guard had grown tired of hearing him drone on about the thorn but had politely said nothing. They loved Willie and could endure his enthusiasms. Not everyone in the walls of St. John's had such patience.

Father Timothy had arrived at his office that morning to see a parishioner camped outside in the hall. He recognized her immediately. A few days earlier, the old lady had interrogated him about her dead dog: whether it would be saved, had been condemned to hell, or was sentenced to an animal limbo until judgment day. He agreed to pray for the dog's repose but said he couldn't be so bold as to pronounce whether the dog had been saved. He promised he'd look into the matter and investigate official church doctrine.

Now confronted with the prospects of having to publicly acknowledge he'd failed in his mission, or that his promise itself was silly, he took evasive action. Convinced himself he was not in the mood for such a confrontation this morning. Fortunately, he had spotted her down the long hallway to his office, and he had quickly turned around and left undetected. He figured he would get a cup of coffee and a paper and then return to work an hour later. He was in the process of taking the longer exit route from the building, one that led him through the church itself, when he bumped into Willie in the threshold of the Amsterdam entrance.

"Willie! I'm so sorry. I didn't see you. How are you doing, today?"

"Good, Father. How are you?"

"Well, indeed. What brings you to church so early this morning?"

"They're planting the thorn."

"Of course," he answered, remembering the occasion and genuinely touched by Willie's devotion. "When does the ceremony begin?" he looked at his watch out of habit.

"Not for another hour. I figured you'd be there, Father."

Father Timothy hated these types of situations where circumstances seemed to conspire to portray him as somehow negligent in his duties or lacking in proper piety. In truth, he had not been scheduled to be present at the ceremony, but he didn't feel like explaining his schedule and thought that sharing a small confession with Willie might disarm his interlocuter. "To tell you the truth Willie," he said confidingly, "I'm not too big on the crown of thorns, relics, stigmata, the grail, and the like. It makes for good reading. I used to love Tennyson's tales. My grandmother gave me a complete edition for my twelfth birthday. Read them all the time. So many years ago. But I don't want to keep you from the planting. When did you say it was?"

"Not until ten."

"Oh, yes," he said, again looking at his watch and realizing it would provide no relief this time. Willie took the lull in talk as an opportunity to speak, and he did so, though somewhat nervously and cautiously so as not to be overheard by passersby entering and leaving the church.

"Father, I saw him again last night."

He tried to judge Father Timothy's reaction to this revelation to see if he should continue, but he saw nothing. Desperate for a response, he ventured on.

"On the roof of the Cathedral House. He was staring out toward the park. Then he ran along the rooftop to the east, jumped into a tree, and reappeared a minute or so later on top of the school. Then he disappeared again."

Father Timothy stared blankly at him, and then a look of pity came across his face.

"I saw him the night before, too. Or heard him. I'm not sure if I saw him. But I saw something on the Deanery. I guess I can't say for sure what it was. But I heard something. Around one o'clock, or so."

"Willie, please, for heaven's sake. I assure you, there is no ape. No beast on the loose in the church. Animal protection has taken care of everything. You have nothing to worry about. Now, please, enough of this talk. People will think you're not well. I don't want them to think that. You're my dear friend."

"I just thought you should know. The people should know."

"Willie, I do know. There's absolutely nothing. Trust me."

"Well, I thought, you know, if there's any danger or what."

"Willie, not again."

"You heard about the killing, didn't you?" he asked, referring to a story that had been in the paper the previous day. "That prostitute. Beaten to death down on West 38th. How do you know it's not that ape? A guy in the next room said he heard something, heard strange animal noises. Not human. People are talking."

"Willie, enough. And let me ask you, how good is the word of a man who frequents such a place? He probably did it himself. And what does a prostitute know? Can the word of such a person be trusted? People will always talk. It's human nature. I am sorry that a whore died, but an ape didn't kill her. You mustn't blame an animal for the deeds of a very sick and ignorant man. And unfortunately, we have thousands of them in the city. My guess is they keep the whorehouses in business. Anyhow, an animal can't be a murderer, can't do evil. You can't blame the animal world for this. You need free will and a conscience to be a murderer, you see, and therefore your beast wouldn't qualify, would he?"

Willie was a little knocked off balance by Father Timothy's aggressive tone of voice, but managed a reply. "But, well, who, or what, knows the evil they do at the time? I know I don't."

"Nonsense, Willie. You don't do evil. And neither do I. Nor does any other self-respecting person. All this talk of evil, Willie, it's utter nonsense," he said, shaking his head. "Do you know what I think?" he continued, conscious that a more conciliatory tone might put an end to his parishioner's concerns. "I think there's no evil. Only ignorance." He hesitated to judge Willie's response, then continued, encouraged. "Now ignorance is a very dangerous thing, indeed, but it's not evil. Ignorance is a better description of our human shortcomings. It explains our foibles without sounding too demeaning. We've spent hundreds of years shedding such benighted ideas like evil. Ignorance is our foe, Willie. Not some beast running on the rooftops of our church. What do you think of that?"

Willie was a little confused.

"Don't you see? There's no evil. No ape. Only ignorance. Fortunately for us, we can combat this foe. We know where he lives."

Father Timothy felt Willie was coming over to his side, but he needed to close the deal, so he continued passionately.

"And our job, yours and mine, is to put an end to ignorance. And we begin this task right here, in Morningside Heights. We begin by volunteering in the community. Doing the kind of good works you've done for our church for so many years. The kind of good works I deeply appreciate. Making sure every young person gets as good an education as possible. If we can do that, we put an end to all of our troubles. What do you think, Willie? Are you with me?"

Somewhat hesitantly, Willie nodded. "I'm with you."

"Good. And now that we've identified our foe, ferreted him forth from his hiding place, described his habits and brought him to bay, let's drive him from our world and put an end to him once and for all. No rational person would intentionally do evil, Willie, and so no one would *ever* do evil. End ignorance, and we end this so called evil. And you and I are joined together on this quest. The better we understand ignorance, the more thoroughly we describe its habits and practices, the better equipped we are for defeating it. And the way to understand it is at the grassroots level. In cities like New York. In neighborhoods like ours. You can't do it in some ivory tower or classroom. You and I, Willie, we're the boots on the ground, going door to door. We're the ones in the field, taking notes, serving soup, saving souls. We've seen the face of ignorance. Can describe it to a tee. And that's how we'll end its reign. Usher in a better tomorrow. And there, my good friend, is your new millennium."

Willie was silent.

"Good, then we're agreed, my friend. No more talk of such non-sense."

Then Father Timothy added sincerely, "I need you Willie. I depend on you." Willie felt a little awkward at his priest's confession, yet he was a little flattered too. Still, he remained troubled. Both reason and experience told him there was real evil in the world. The events of the twentieth century told him so, loudly and clearly. Events he knew all too well. He wanted to voice his concern without insulting Father Timothy.

"But," Willie stammered looking beyond Father Timothy's head and into the bustling street behind him. "But, what if…"

"But what, Willie? What don't you understand?"

"But what if ignorance… can't a… can a bad description of evil itself be evil? Be the greatest evil?"

It seemed obvious to Father Timothy that Willie had not followed his train of thought, had not bought into this idea of their partnership, but he was at a loss about how to further to explain it. He was saved from floundering by his cell phone, though, which chirped before the silence became too awkward. "Praise God for technology," he thought. The call was of little importance, but Father Timothy realized it as an opportunity. He answered the call, and his exaggerated reaction and tone of voice suggested it was a matter of impressive gravity. He turned the mouthpiece aside, smiled at Willie, and waved him off whispering. "It's very important business, Willie. We'll talk again. Come see me sometime. Don't be a stranger. Now onward, Willie! Onward!" And with that he descended the steps toward Amsterdam, and Willie quietly made to enter the church.

~~~~~

WHENEVER POSSIBLE, HE LUNCHED in front of Alice's statue. Three, four times a week. It was a good people watching spot. Today, he had not heard English spoken by parkgoers for some ten minutes, a span which confirmed his view that the place was being overrun not only by Madison Avenue but by foreigners. In a flash of insight, he realized how badly he wanted them all gone. Permanently. When he finished lunch he made his way down by the boathouse and to the Terrace, which overlooked the pond like some sort of gateway. He thought it more of a hellmouth, framing the gondoliers and rowboats beyond. As carefully planned as any building in the city, the park had its own economy and logic—and yet there was also much of it that was left unaccounted for. And every day he came here to consider how man had tried to impose order on nature and how man had failed.

Olmstead had employed as many as 4,000 workers tilling the soil at one time, planted over 600,000 shrubs, dug lakes, burrowed hillocks, and arranged acres of flowers, all in an effort to subdue and mold eight hundred acres. He believed his paradise could rival the Catskills and Adirondacks. Keep the tourist and their dollars at home. He was right. Citizens came here for entertainment, for pleasure, for spiritual refreshment—lured by a menagerie of nature's attractions. An unprecedented variety of flora and fauna was available to all. The range of trees was astonishing, as were the over five hundred types of birds. There were also squirrels, rabbits, possum—and lately, according to rumors and a few tabloid headlines, a chimp. Had it not been for the Yankees' roll through the playoffs and the Rangers' quick start, the media would have converged on the park in full force, scouring the garden for the apeman some late-night joggers claimed to have seen.

But of all the species rumored to be about the place it was the birds that most interested Lynch. Nearly six months before, he'd been heading up town at the end of a long day to keep an appointment he had made to examine some property an uncle was considering purchasing, when a sparrow fell to the earth before his feet at the precise moment he realized his cell phone was dead. Instinctively, he kicked the bird aside, an act that earned him the reproach of an old lady who'd witnessed his reaction. He smiled at her righteousness, considering his options. There was no time for violence. So gently picking the bird up, he placed it on a nearby bench. Incredibly, it immediately took flight. He shrugged his shoulders, as if to say "I've done my part," then walked on. He would soon realize that indulging his elder had been a costly mistake; he arrived at the platform just as his train was taking off. Though it meant he'd be cutting his appointment close, he had no alternative but to hail a cab at this most disagreeable of hours.

When he finally made it to the apartment, he was thirty minutes late and the agent had left. Returning to the street, he was again confronted with the task of hailing a cab during rush hour. This time his bad luck was compounded, for it had begun to rain. Not wanting his suit to get damaged, he decided to seek shelter in the nearest building. Unfortunately, hundreds of others had had the same thought, and every diner he sought to enter was packed, forcing him elsewhere.

And so he eventually found himself in the immense nave of St. John's. The cathedral amazed him, for he had not even heard of its existence. Yet here it was, rising three hundred feet above the street on a bluff in Harlem. He decided to return the next night. The sheer scope of the church's vision impressed him for it seemed archaic, and yet the artwork inside intrigued, especially the stained glass and sculpture. There, within the fold of the church—ordered by its inspired architecture—were birds, stags, dragons and wolves. Even whales and peacocks.

Yet as he made his way through the vacant church that first night, with the sound of his leather-soled Lobbs echoing along the flagstone, he could not help but think the church was off key. Something struck him as dissonant. Still he returned the next night. And then again. The repeated visits to the cathedral led to an invitation to attend an art appreciation class that allowed students to dabble in the arts that comprised the cathedral. And it was at such a class when he overheard a fellow student mention the most unique celebration in the cathedral's calendar: the blessing of the animals on the Feast Day of St. Francis. And it was on that occasion that he'd witnessed a most memorable performance. His own. He smiled as he thought back upon the chaotic scene. Then he finished off his sandwich and headed back to work, which he wouldn't leave until after ten.

~~~~~

THAT NIGHT WILLIE MADE A pilgrimage to the cathedral, which he'd often do so as to enjoy its beauty in silence and solitude. But this evening he also went to admire some of the most recently completed statuary, Simon Verity's stone work on the Portal of Paradise, as it was captured in a small documentary photo exhibit. He'd seen workers setting up the large black and white photos on easels in a small bay off the nave the previous afternoon. He wanted to avoid the crowds and knew coming at night would accomplish that. But the truth was he also wanted to walk the cathedral grounds alone, investigating something he'd overheard a cashier at the bookstore mention: that there'd been some unusual damage to a gargoyle on a buttress at the southeast end of the Close. He didn't think he'd be able to get near enough to the figure to inspect it, and he knew he was no expert at assessing damage, but he instinctively felt compelled to try. He owed it to the cathedral.

The cashier had told a few of the cathedral's maintenance workers that the figure was obscured by a large oak, and that she'd overheard a workman saying there was no way it could be the result of weather and yet that it looked too significant to be the work of squirrels or possums. Willie quietly took in the exchange, and left the store without even being noticed. But the conspiracy theorist in Willie quietly wondered if it could be the work of an ape. Or a man wielding a chisel. He mulled over the irony that a man might use a chisel to destroy, turning presence into absence, when its purpose was the exact opposite: to the render the eternal, making forever present that which is absent. He ceased this train of thought as he neared the cathedral. Stopping at the intersection of 113th and Amsterdam, he gazed upward at the noble structure in the distance, admiring its façade and tower that reached up to the low-hanging fog that had rolled in from the Hudson, a quarter mile to the west. He felt humbled to be a tiny part of the history of the structure. Being part of an effort that had endured generations brought him a level of peace he received from no other of his activities. He smiled and continued on toward the monument to John of Patmos.

In childhood, he'd been terrified of the church—of the loud noises involved in its construction and then later of its grotesque and disfigured form which, at dawn and dusk, cast the whole neighborhood in a lengthened shadow as cool as a morgue. As a young man, he was uncertain whether the church should not have been killed in its inception rather than be allowed to suffer into its misshapen existence, for though he'd witnessed decades of its life, its shape didn't seem to be moving toward resolution or even anything resembling harmony. In fact, a paradox had seemed at work, for more effort than ever appeared to be needed to complete the task. But now, as an old man, having lived a full life of joy and sorrow, he'd come to love its awkward profile, finding comfort in its ever-present scaffolding and familiar asymmetries. Now, he never wandered out of its sight, still a considerable radius given the church's location on a bluff in Morningside Heights and the tower's three hundred feet. Willie especially loved to visit the cathedral at night. This passion had allowed him to develop a close bond with the night security team, especially Anthony, the watchman of the Close and west entrance.

"Come to see your house, Willie?" his old friend asked.

"Yeah—come to see *our* house."

Anthony smiled. "You gonna finish it soon?"

"Oh, man, not soon enough."

"For real? When you do think?"

"Not in my lifetime."

"Aren't you working those boys hard enough, Willie?" he asked chuckling. "You sure you putting in long enough hours?"

"Pretty long. At least we were. Until June, they had four of us working on some statues for the northern tower. But man, they hanged to machines, mainly. Digital cameras. Robot saws. And they broke down last month and haven't been fixed. All they got me doing now is giving tours. Picard and Verity went back to Europe to look at some new equipment. But I don't expect we'll get back to carving any time soon. Saving money though, I guess."

"That's what it's all about these days, isn't it?"

"That's what they tell me. And I just do what I'm told," he replied. And with that comment, a tip of his cap and a friendly smile, he gained admission to the nave, walked briefly through the exhibit—he'd come back to it on his way out, he thought to himself—and made his way to the southern tower's entrance. Unbeknownst to him, he would be the third to climb the tower that night.

~~~~~

FORTY MINUTES, THREE STAIRWELLS, AND 124 spiral steps later, he reached the tower's arcade and stood in silence, gazing south toward midtown three and half miles away. The thickening fog now fully obscured the earth, some 250 feet below, but not the rooftops of any buildings of over a dozen stories. The moon shone brightly, giving the cloudy canopy a heaving, rolling appearance which was punctured at regular intervals by the flying buttresses and pinnacles that rose along the side of the vaulted nave. Cram's Gothic adaptation to LaFarge's original Romanesque design was pleasing and an admirable example of man's ability to change course, and Willie stared out upon the scene, instinctively moved by its strange beauty if not fully understanding its architectural significance or knowing all of its 108 year history. Like most of its admirers and congregants, he was oblivious to the facts that its construction had begun hardly a year after the frontier was declared closed, that Astors and Morgans and Vanderbilts had contributed to its coffers, and that nine thousand worshippers could easily gather in its enormous interior, beneath its forty foot rose window, to praise God and petition for the forgiveness of sins.

Neither was he aware that at that moment the ape, hidden from any pedestrians on the other side of the fog's veil, was moving gracefully along a flying buttress and scaling a pinnacle not thirty yards off. Only when the beast began to clap its hands and hoot, pointing a bony finger toward the moon and then the eastern side of the tower, was Willie's attention redirected from his aesthetic contemplation. He followed the direction of the beast's gesture but saw nothing. And when the beast suddenly descended and headed back across the stone bridge and toward the roof of the nave, Willie went to investigate. Moving through the darkness of the tower's interior platform, he banged his knees on tool boxes and nearly fell on his face twice, bumping into buckets and hoses and slowly making his way among stored scaffolding and assorted hardware. The tower's construction had been halted a dozen years before when it was determined that donations should be spent upon maintenance rather than additional construction, and yet much of the building equipment had merely been stored in place rather than returned to earth, and it was proving a challenge to navigate. Willie finally emerged in an aperture near the southeastern corner of the tower's arcade, as close as he could get to where he thought the ape had been headed, yet looking out at the buttress, he again saw nothing.

But then he heard something, the unmistakable panting sound of a chimp at play, coming from around a corner, just out of sight. He stepped onto the southern-facing ledge of the arcade, one that looked down upon the Close, and as the fog began to thicken and rise, slowly edged his way toward the noise.

~~~~~

FROM THE EASTERN LEDGE of the same tower, another figure moved, as well, and as he reached the tower's corner, saw the chimp balanced on the head of a gargoyle—a bloated and tonsured monk— playfully tapping its bald pate. A mist now washed over both forms, obscuring where one ended and the other began. And as the broad shape stepped out onto the arm of stone that supported the gargoyle, he saw out of the corner of his eye another figure stepping blindly toward the same space, its attention fixed on the beast. Instinctively, he drove the chisel deep into this shorter figure's throat and, with a firm push, sent him hurtling into the abyss.

As he raced headlong toward the archangel, and in the split second before he lost consciousness, Willie looked up and into the face of the man he'd warned Father Timothy about for three months. His gaze was not met, though, for Lynch had already turned to face the beast. But the ape had vanished. Never to be seen again.

He would hear its hoots and yips and cackles, though. All night long. He spent the next three hours searching the tower for the beast, even venturing out onto the roof of the nave, then the Deanery and School, in pursuit of the animal. To no end. The taunts and mocking laughter echoed across the rooftops of Morningside Heights, descending madly—wheeling and swirling and finally diving down from the gothic spires and into the streets of Gotham and toward a small statue in a distant park, as if summoned by the right hand of nonsense itself.

~~~~~

FOR THE FIRST TIME IN WEEKS he'd slept well. Father Timothy woke early, made a pot of coffee, read the paper for an hour, then headed to work, determined to give a call to the distraught owner of the recently departed pet whom he had so determinedly avoided the previous day.

He caught a cab uptown but on an impulse got out a half mile from the church; though it was cold, the sun was rising, and it was too nice of a morning to ride inside a cab. Cabs were forms of mass escape, he mused. And such unconscious strategies of evasion were part of the city's problems, he contended quietly to himself while walking north on Amsterdam. A blustery wind moved across the face of the city. There was a fair amount of traffic on the sidewalks, even though it was only 6:45. Vendors were setting up their carts, owners were rummaging through store fronts—arranging magazines, fruits, and merchandise—and college students filled window booths and sipped coffee while discussing politics. Father Timothy smiled as the neighborhood wiped sleep from its eyes and prepared to meet the late October day.

As he passed by the tree-shaded entrance to the cathedral Close, a violent rush of wind burst forth from the courtyard, momentarily bracing him, and an object skittered out onto the sidewalk before his feet. Unawares, Father Timothy had actually kicked it twice before even realizing something was wrong. Because it was more substantial than the usual offal that perpetually circulated around the city streets, he stooped down to pick it up. It was a cap. He brushed the cap against his thigh twice and turned it right side out. It was a Yankees cap. Like the one Willie wore.

Father Timothy recalled Willie had been wearing it the previous day when he'd been feeding the birds at the statue. Thinking perhaps Willie had left a backpack or some other objects on one of the benches surrounding the archangel, he went to investigate.

Entering the acre of garden from the street, his attention was immediately drawn to a shape near the base of the tower. A shape that did not belong there. He walked the short distance to the crumpled form, his confusion growing with each step. Kneeling down beside the figure, he extended his hand and felt along the neck for a pulse. But he knew the person had not slept here beside a shrub in the Close. Knew the body had fallen from the sky. Father Timothy looked up toward the tower's top. Three hundred feet above him. He imagined the fall: a tear of wax down the side of a candle, but his aesthetic sense was disturbed by a squirrel which began licking about the dark stain that shadowed the figure. He began to feel faint. Minutes passed. It seemed to Father Timothy that his stranger had finally made a visit. Delivering a message he would not soon forget. He saw then the cost of his naivete. The price was laid out before him, and it was considerable. Everything.

With a tug, more strenuous than he'd expected to need, he removed the chisel from his friend's throat. Staring vacantly at the blood-soaked implement, he tossed it aside and then slowly made his way around the statue to one of the stone benches.

A half hour passed. On the sidewalk and street not twenty yards from the archangel, students were now walking to class. Horns blared out their displeasure, shop doors opened for business, a wind snapped the awnings of a dozen diners, hustling its way through the streets of the great city. But here at the Cathedral of St. John the Divine, the earth no longer seemed to wheel through space. Here in the cathedral Close, earth had found a new pole, with an axis extending through its surface from the end of the archangel's sword. Here now before him, the lone still point around which his new world must forever turn.

It was then that Timothy Washburn's cell phone began to chirp, and as if on cue, a host of small birds, sparrows, skipped up before him, heads bobbing, only to turn about with misgiving. Yet he only looked up from the blood on his hands when he heard a small object fall to the ground before him. He looked closely to be sure it was what he thought it was. A shoe. A laceless shoe. It landed in the shadow of a large object that hung from the great wing of the statue and swayed slightly in the cold air. He looked up from the shoe, into the source of the darkness, and then back down to the ground before him. And the shoe became a splotch, and the splotch resolved itself into the shade of a great, iron wing.

~~~~~

For many years to come, he would wander the grounds of this church on a hill. Out of habit, one he could not break, he would look into the night sky for a sign. But there was no sign—no sign save a beast on the loose in an unfinished church.

The Dead Watch

Henry Adams sat alone and cried silently at the song sung by the painted whore. It was the third day in a row he had managed to slip away from his nurse and catch a cab from the Rue Bonaparte to the foot of Montmartre to see the burlesque show. Miss Aileen Tone had vowed only that morning not to let her aged charge slip away into the Paris crowd during his noontime stroll in the Tuileries Gardens. Despite her best intentions, Adams had vanished.

He had begun to relish the part of stealing away to the cabaret. There was a certain rush that accompanied this assertion of will, a certain pleasure had from the decisiveness required to do something others did not want him to do. It was neither the brassy music nor the nimble dancers that lured him there. Nor was it the mirrored halls, the pretentious art exhibitions, or the outlandishly costumed chimps who performed daily. It was the whore. He felt almost depraved succumbing to the charms of the twenty year old, a Creole from New Orleans by way of Baltimore who had run away from poverty three years earlier and who had of late become the talk of both polite, Parisian society and the small circle of American expatriates Adams was fond of referring to mockingly as his band of "improvised Europeans."

Not that any of them would deign to set foot in such a club, though. In the summer of 1914, Paris was at the height of its decadence and cabarets such as Le Coq Perdu throbbed with libertine activity, the kind to which no self-respecting expatriate would be party. American dilettantes could be terrible gossips, but they typically did little more than shyly observe such proceedings from a distance. But not Adams.

The whore herself had become more than a little curious at the behavior of her oldest admirer. Indeed, even the club's manager had at first suspected Adams might be another agent from the police morals unit, sent in undercover to record illegal activity. These suspicions were soon dispelled by Adams' benign behavior. He would arrive early, securing the best table in the house. After checking his pocket watch, as if in confirmation of an appointment time, he would procure a magnet and iron filings from a slender cigar case tucked inside his coat. He would then fidget about with the trinkets, hunched contentedly over the mysterious movement his ancient hands orchestrated. This struck many onlookers as peculiar, but Adams was a man at home with contradiction, so long as it was not the product of undisciplined thought processes. When the whore stepped forth to begin her routine, he sat back up, perfectly still, rapt with attention. He made no lewd gestures or catcalls, only gazed out at her like some benevolent, exhausted, sexless presence, oblivious to the cacophony of shouts and the flow of alcohol, making of the thick cigar smoke about him—it had struck more than one patron—a dim cowl.

Miss Tone had warned him about the adverse effects of smoke on his constitution. She had grown especially protective of Adams even before his vision had begun to fail him, when the unsettling incident in the bakery had occurred a month earlier, and he had lost control of his French while waiting to buy a baguette. Watched helplessly as the words left his mind as if water through cupped hand. But his French returned—he had found himself only momentarily dumb-stricken—and he could see well enough, thanks to the reading glasses Miss Tone had recently procured for him. Indeed, the occasionally bespectacled Adams soon developed the habit of withdrawing his pocket watch from his waist coat, adjusting his glasses as he severely eyed the watch, and then—with an exaggerated expression of surprise at what he saw, as if to convince any onlooker that his eyesight was indeed good enough to read time—returning it abruptly to his waist coat and determinedly walking off as if he were late to a meeting.

Miss Tone knew his mannerisms quite well and supposed she had less to worry about than she sometimes thought. Eventually, she had come to realize the impossibility of her situation, anyhow, for none could contain Adams. He had always had the ability to come and go as he pleased. It was the birthright of this descendant of presidents.

And the truth of the matter was that even at his age he could maneuver nimbly through the narrow canyons of the city's tenements as
deftly as he could the political cabals of Washington and the folios of
medieval chansons from Mont Saint Michel, whose translation had
of late become his passion, an office to which he devoted himself with
singular intensity.

Whether conjugating an archaic verb from middle French or negotiating for vegetables in the market, Adams always moved with élan
and grace, and appeared to come out the winner, even to those haggling
farmers who'd actually bested him. For some reason, natives deferred
to him without realizing it or knowing why. To them he seemed less an
American and more some hoary anachronism gone astray, wandered
out of the distant past and into the present. The petty venders who set
up their stalls in the Latin Quarter on market day had actually grown
wary of this diminutive figure. Some had even become so superstitious
of his presence that they shrank from him in a manner not unlike that
of their ancestors, peasants who had lunged back from the passing
coach of Erasmus, recently arrived at the Sorbonne for disputation and
the condemnation of some new heresy.

Although Adams hadn't arrived in Paris to burn heretics or con-
sign infidels to hell—in truth it was his conviction that no one believed in anything anymore, including heaven or hell—Miss Tone had
noticed the strange behavior Adams invoked in others. However, she
had exercised sound judgment and said nothing to him about it. She
did not wish to upset him. She only wished he would not disappear
on her watch. But this, too, she felt could not be blamed on him, for
he always returned to the apartments, cheerful and refreshed, after
several hours. The combination of his impish grin and a thoughtfully
chosen word always seemed to disarm her and serve as sufficient
penance. No servants dared ask him where he'd been, but they would
conspire after hours, vowing to double their efforts so as not to lose
sight of their charge. It was more than a staff of five could manage,
however, and they were beginning to feel themselves overmatched by
the seventy-six year old.

On this particular afternoon, Adams returned precisely at 2:00 PM,
took an early tea, informing Miss Tone that he would be driving out to
Chartres in an hour and for her to make the necessary arrangements.

He retired to his apartments without further comment. Miss Tone was surprised. It was the first time in weeks that Adams did not seek an update regarding the excavations of the Dordogne caves outside Les Eyzies that he was helping to finance. He had previously shown the greatest enthusiasm for this dim and chill warehouse of the past, where five years previous a teenage goatherd had stumbled upon the priceless treasures while tending his flock. A team of scholars funded by Adams was helping to preserve and study the site, the oldest such one in Europe, where early man had first scribbled his pictures on stone walls. Indeed, Adams had gone so far as to cultivate a close relationship with Henri Hubert, the distinguished Director of the National Ethnology Museum and an archaeologist of great renown. In return for Adams' generous benefaction, Hubert had secretly agreed to grant his unusual request: that if the bones of a prehistoric child were dug up, they would be delivered to Adams.

But even more surprising to Miss Tone than this apparent neglect for the caves was the fact that Adams would not be spending the afternoon working with his nieces on his beloved medieval chansons. He had not even inquired about the progress they'd made that morning in their researches. For the past seven years, Adams had concentrated a large portion of his energies on translating these twelfth and thirteenth century relics, seeking to decipher the accompanying musical notation he'd unearthed in church and state archives.

After the publication of his book, his passion had shifted from the windows at Chartres to the songs sung at Mont Saint Michel during the golden age of Normandy, the years following William's conquest of England. Pilgrims had flocked to the holy site then, welcomed by the Benedictine monks who allowed, and even encouraged, the performance of mystery plays and the singing of medieval romances. More than one legend suggested that these medieval songs had the restorative power of an elixir and were themselves as sought after as the grail itself. So for three months each year, Adams escaped the oppressively hot Washington summer, turning his back on the capital and immersing himself in the study of this arcanum. He fancied these chansons his surrogate children, trapped in a silent limbo, and conceived of his research as a sort of midwifery, a sacred duty to give life again to these living, breathing entities, deliver them from their grim consignment. A secret part of him hoped that his efforts and decency might someday be similarly rewarded, if the occasion so required and he were likewise consigned to oblivion.

For according to Adams' calculations, no human ear had heard the songs properly sung in over five hundred years. For half a millennium, they had lain in darkness, awaiting resurrection. Were themselves a sort of color yet undiscovered. A continent shrouded in mystery, awaiting revelation. This calculation was supported by the work of Adams' colleague and close friend Heinrich Mueller, a thoroughly anglicized German scholar of the Middle Ages and Professor in Oxford whom Adams had been in close correspondence with for the past two years and whose work he also helped finance. The two had been friends ever since Adams' student days in Berlin. Mueller himself was a disciple of Leopold on Ranke, and though Adams had grown skeptical of Ranke's scientific approach to history, he had sent Mueller all his latest findings on the chansons in hopes of attaining additional insight. The two had been working more closely on the chansons this summer. In fact, Mueller's latest correspondence had hinted that he was on the verge of a breakthrough. To achieve the noble end of recovering the sound of these silent works, the two friends had set about studying Gregorian chants, modal harmonies, and the primitive musical notation of the twelfth century. Adams had long harbored a pet theory—a prejudice, really—that the *Chanson de Roland* was a Norman song usurped later by the French, and he was determined to prove his hypothesis correct.

More close to his heart, though, was recovering the melody of Richard the Lion Heart's *Prison Song*, the most celebrated court song of the Middle Ages, an epoch Adams believed to be infinitely better proportioned and healthier than his own. Legend related that the song attributed to the heroic crusader had moved popes to tears and elicited fits of repentance from more than one king. Adams himself had grown suspicious that his song might well be the supreme achievement of mankind. Separating Adams from this cherished song was an inscrutable system of musical notation, one he'd wrestled with so long that he interpreted its existence as a personal affront, a veritable Rosetta Stone whose hidden code concealed a tongue unknown practically since the dispersal at Babylon.

To aid him in his endeavors, Adams had recruited the usual, capable coterie of nieces whose intellects were most formidable and whose loyalty was unquestioned. A seminar room had been improvised from a parlor in his apartments on the Left Bank, and stacks of dusty documents, folios, reference works and a fantastic assortment of impractical, ancient instruments—calipers and scales and tweezers and magnifying glasses—lined the shelves. During his months in Paris, his arrival in the seminar room was punctilious, his hours of work long and arduous, concluding only after he sensed the sunset through the drawn window blinds, a suspicion he would confirm with a glance at his pocket watch. The routine adhered to a clockwork precision, which comforted Adams with a sort of illusory control to his days. But the truth was that Adams had of late grown desperate to make headway into Richard's *Song* and was hoping Mueller might revive his enthusiasm. He was quickly growing bored with his menagerie of trinkets and manuscripts, no matter how much visitors were awed by the spectacle of the curious parlor.

Perhaps most impressive of all, though—and certainly most flattering to Miss Tone—was the Steinway in the center of the seminar room. Adams had purchased the piano for the purpose of helping to unriddle melodies. Miss Tone, whose father taught music at Clongowes, had the enviable assignment of trying to recapture in performance the melodies Adams worked out on paper. In less than a week after his arrival in Paris, he had converted the room into a sort of research lab whose products were sounded upon this priceless touchstone. Adams and his nieces would critique Tone's play, suggesting alterations and scribbling frantically in their notebooks with each touch of key. Once a week, Miss Tone would deliver a concert of recovered songs before an audience of expatriates, government officials, and other assorted friends. On rare occasions, when the moment took him, Adams himself would sing a song with his fine tenor, much to the delight of his company. This gave Miss Tone great pleasure.

And these were the fond memories she was running through her head when she set out for the driver's quarters and informed him to prepare the car for Adams. Mr. Foulkestone narrowed his liver-colored eyes upon hearing her instructions. He looked at his watch and cursed beneath his breath, but not too loudly, for he knew Miss Tone's loyalty and compassion exceeded his own. Still, he hated the idea of a long drive—a glorified joyride, really—one whose unlikely hour of departure would require a return trip after nightfall. Nor had he ever warmed to Adams' occasional jabs at the royal family. Although Foulkestone was of middling birth, he never appreciated such comments from an American. Nonetheless, after shaving—and then ironing and donning his uniform—he headed over to the garage.

To Adams, though, it was no joyride, but a pilgrimage. And his car was no toy, but a sort of sanctuary, a gas-propelled tabernacle. It was true Adams adored his car. He confessed his love freely. He loved the warm whir and clank of dynamo as it subdued the mysteries of space and time and delivered distant cathedrals to the running board of his Model T. Countless times he had bored visitors to his apartment with talk of the car's four cylinder, four stroke motor, complete with flywheel magneto and removable cylinder head. He bragged about the tires, the gear box, and the top speed of forty miles an hour. "Better than any horse at Ascot," he was fond of saying, "and easier to clean up after." He rejoiced at the very thought of having so much power at his command; he took great pride in the chrome pipes, the intricate grillwork, the leather seats, and the cacophony which signaled his imminent approach like the stampede of armored steeds. He admitted he enjoyed nothing more than driving through the Norman landscape, scattering dogs and children, blowing past hay wains and belching out a sooty smoke into the azure sky above the poppy fields.

More than one casual observer had remarked that as Adams' own facility for locomotion diminished, his adoration for the machine increased. Even a beloved niece suspected that what had begun as a diversion had become an obsession. Indeed, one night Miss Tone, disturbed from her sleep by fearful premonitions, went to check Adams' apartments and found them vacant. Not wishing to alarm the household, she continued her search alone and eventually discovered Adams just before dawn, in the garage and on his knees before the powerful machine, meticulously polishing the car's chrome fender and headlight casings while still in his night gown. She took his hand, helped him up, and quietly returned him to his room, choosing not to report the incident to his nieces.

The truth was that though he could still, on occasion, move as nimbly as any pickpocket—taking a high curb with a dancer's grace or slipping through the doors of a lift at the last possible moment—Adams had grown aware that he was aging, and in moments of weakness, secretly dreamed of being doted on. He believed he had succeeded in disguising this impulse from others, though. Nonetheless, this awareness would have saddened any countryman who had had the privilege of knowing the young Adams, a man of unsurpassed charm, wit, and ambition who had once been the most sought after dinner companion and dancing partner in all of Washington.

But that was long ago, and now Adams, situating himself in the backseat of his car, anxiously consulted his pocket watch before unfolding the table tray before him and taking out his magnet and iron filings. The three-hour drive would be taken up by this occult diversion and the rich backdrop of manor houses and farms. And the whore's song. Adams could not get it out of his head. He had not been so taken since his South Sea wanderings and Tahitian sojourn, where the songs sung him by Marau Taaroa, the island's ancient and final queen, recounted a lost and noble history he had imaginatively transcribed. Adams still counted the regal, old woman a close friend, one of the most impressive persons he had ever met.

But the whore was more bewitching still. Her voice was youthful but strong, and though her countenance was defiant, her body was almost frail. She recalled to him the wretched immigrants of his native land, could have been one of the wave of desperate refugees who'd fled from Sherman's advancing army during the bloody conflagration that Adams and his father had tried so desperately to keep America from entering into a half century earlier. In charming contrast to this grim evocation were the melody and lyrics to the song, the latter of which dated from time immemorial and alluded to a popular folktale Adams had come across again and again in the archives while researching the medieval chansons. It was a legend which had long fascinated him.

Though Adams had first heard the lyrics in another of their numerous manifestations, he immediately recognized the whore's version for what it was. His researches into the chansons had given him great pleasure, in part by confirming to him the arbitrary nature of history, its various faces and misleading avenues, its existence as a fabric containing innumerable threads woven tougher, overlapping and inseparable. History was a labyrinth, and Adams had concluded there was no city on earth better suited to conduct research into its serpentine ways than Paris. Most tourists who flocked to the City of Lights at the fin de siècle perceived only the metropolis as it had been redesigned in the mid nineteenth century by Baron Georges Haussman, who had overseen the destruction of many of the city's medieval tenements and its network of narrow, dim alleys, some of whose cobbled surfaces had not seen the light of day since Charlemagne's rule. In their place, Haussman had erected the spacious squares, gardens, and wide boulevards which became home to sidewalk cafes and salons. But Adams saw beneath the bewildering veneer of lights and glitz. In his own travels around town, he could still make out traces of the ancient Roman settlement dating back to the first century A.D., saw evidence of the stone fortifications constructed by Clovis—first ruler of the Frankish kingdom who had made Paris his capital in 507—was unsettled by the echo of ancient disputes still lingering in the courtyards of the thousand year old University, and had on more than one occasion felt deafened by the cacophony of mounted troops who had last paraded beneath the city's great arch built almost a century earlier.

Especially this summer, though, Adams had felt the city to be a living, breathing organism, its past coexisting with its present. He had begun to consider that one abstracted the present, untangled its activity from the past, only at one's own peril. Years of summering in Paris had convinced Adams that the city was a palimpsest upon which had been inscribed the history of the West, a history whose remnants were still visible to the sensitive eye. It struck him as a riot of ghosts and half-buried ruins which he was trying desperately to bring under control. To cast into story. To birth into narrative. Often, he felt himself losing the battle. Nonetheless, he had about concluded that history was always a construct and a working up of legend, and its only justification was its aesthetic quality. A part of him sensed that the whore, ignorant as she was, must have intuitively realized this too: all abstractions, all concepts of historical facts—dried and pinned to a page—must have been foreign to her. She was completely unconscious of the song as existing apart from herself, seemed unaware that its story might not belong solely to her. Would have found the mere suggestion preposterous. Nonsense. And in truth, Adams felt the song could not be stripped from her, dissected with a scalpel, pulled apart piece by piece and labeled. The song was part of the living tissue of history, and of the cabaret and of Paris itself. History was too interconnected for such discrete considerations, too slippery for such clinical examination. There was only a doubling-back, a story crisscrossing itself: one that was written over and over again, times without number. It was impossible to tell where, or even if, it actually began. Like the whore's song, it seemed without origin. Its beginning was, it so often seemed to Adams, lost in darkness.

Her song—the final one with which she'd always conclude her short program—had a fascinating tale to tell. It had made vague reference to a French legend about a certain slave of Joseph of Arimathea who had used an urn to catch some of the blood of Christ as it dripped from his pierced side during the crucifixion. The urn was buried with Joseph in Glastonbury, and later came into the possession of the Knights Templar, in the tiny village of Rothley, during their preparations for the crusades. These Knights, as lore had it, brought the urn to Paris for safekeeping after Jerusalem fell to the infidels. One version of the legend continued that the blood, mixed with local spring water, actually provided the rich color for the acres of stained glass at Beauvais, a cathedral the Templars had secretly financed and helped to construct in the early thirteenth century. Another account confirmed that two drops of blood could color tens of square feet of the highest quality stained glass, a prodigious and profitable yield. Still another thread of the tale insisted that one drop of the blood, in combination with holy water, could cure leprosy, blindness, perhaps death itself. Adams knew all the variants of the story and no more doubted the folktale's account of the composition of the glass than he did a scientist's description of the composition of water.

To Adams, Beauvais itself was a monument to the folly of human presumption and the limits of reason, a sort of scholastic tower of Babel. That the enormous cathedral had collapsed on itself before completion, exposing the faulty foundation of its builders, suggested a moral which Adams had occasionally been interested in elaborating for guests at his dinner parties. The cathedral had never been rebuilt, but ever since then the glass had been treasured and much sought after.

Princes had waged war for single panes, and dowries were sealed with mere fragment and shard. What precious little glass survived was most often hoarded and sequestered in secret locations, though some of the glass eventually made its way into public and was cut and set into rings by dozens of noblemen across Normandy seeking to elevate their renown. One popular account related that English archers had brought back just such holy loot to their island after the victory at Agincourt and set several richly hued pieces into the crowned jewels. Another legend circulated that Huguenots had used fragments of the jeweled glass to ransom those few children spared during the St. Bartholomew Day Massacre. Still another fable had Napoleon conquering Egypt in order to force its most revered jeweler to design an elaborate broach, which the emperor then presented to Josephine on the occasion of their first anniversary. Adams himself was familiar with countless varieties of the folktale and considered none more, or less, authentic, than any other. In truth, he thought most of them quite beautiful and had even spent the better portion of a summer two years back scouring rural French flea markets in search of such a ring.

Yet as charming as the song's lyrics were, it was the melody which stunned Adams. For three days he'd found himself in the thrall of this whore's song. And while heading out to Chartres, it was her song that he hummed the entire way. Much to the dismay of his driver.

But Foulkestone, although a servant, was not without recourse. Having of late grown weary of both his station and his employer, he had discovered subtle ways of unsettling Adams, intuitively disrupting his metaphysical attempts to negotiate some sort of settlement between the Virgin and the dynamo. On the way out of Paris, Foulkestone had taken a circuitous route that would lead them by the Eiffel Tower, built for the 1889 World's Fair and to commemorate the centennial of the Revolution. Glancing into his rearview mirror, Foulkestone observed his passenger look up once from his magnet—vaguely aware that it was taking longer than usual to leave the city limits—consult his pocket watch, and in the process of returning it to his waist coat, catch sight of the tower. Foulkestone smiled, seeing his charge shrink and turn away.

He knew that any reminder of the Revolution was anathema to Adams because it inevitably brought to mind Jefferson. Henry, unlike his great grandfather, had never made peace with the family rival. To Adams, the botched experiment which was the French Revolution had been largely the handiwork of a Virginian slave owner possessed of an understanding of human nature the Adams clan had scorned since even before their earliest ancestor had arrived in the Massachusetts Bay.

Adams glanced back out the car window and bit down on his lower lip. Although half a world, and a full century, separated him from Jefferson, his shadow could not be escaped. Adams shook his head and gnashed his teeth. In truth, he had always thought the tower vulgar, a prop for postcards, the supreme expression of soulless industry, of technology divorced from proper end. It struck him then as an abomination, the very antithesis of Chartres. For a mere week's pay, a factory worker could take one of the Otis elevators to the top of the tower. There, a thousand feet above the city, the Parisian could be momentarily freed from the limits of his perspective, could even—to an extent—play God. Indeed, at that moment the tower seemed to Adams a fitting tribute to the Revolution's ill-conceived program of reform and liberation. Passion without check; knowledge without soul. Truth pursued to such an extreme end that it became a falsehood. But what the tower seemed to promise only Chartres could deliver. Or could have delivered, a thousand years ago. So Adams thought, as he sank back down into his seat and returned his attention to the magnet.

They arrived at the cathedral within an hour of dusk. Adams did not wait for the door to be opened for him, but ambled out of the car, stuffed a dozen francs into Foulkestone's hand, mumbled something about a café a few blocks away in the town center, and then headed toward the windows. An hour later, his driver found him in silent rapture before a series of windows centered around a crucifixion scene. Foulkestone was uncertain why his employer had stopped before this window and not one of the more celebrated rose windows, for all this pane of glass seemed to depict was a young man standing in front of the cross, holding out an urn beneath the stigmata. Yet Adams stood before scene in reverential silence, marveling at the window and how it colored the light within the vaulted interior.

Adams harbored a deep suspicion—a vain one, he was willing to acknowledge in the right company—that he alone, of all the cathedral's admirers, was appropriately sensitive to the inadequacy of language before the windows. No dialectic could reduce the fenestration. No syllogism could account for the interrelation of the cathedral's parts. Adams knew that no historians had ever been able to explain Chartres or agree on its significance. Ultimately, all fell mute in the Virgin's presence. Words became unclean in Her temple.

A good ten minutes passed before the driver finally summoned the courage to speak. "It is an impressive window, Mr. Adams."

Adams, who had not heard Foulkestone approach from behind, remained silent.

"I wonder what price the window would fetch on today's market. What do you think, Mr. Adams?"

Adams was elsewhere. After a minute of silence, he spoke—more of a musing aloud or a reply than an attempt to engage in conversation.

"You think we've progressed from here?"

"I beg your pardon, sir?"

"I think not."

"No sir, Mr. Adams."

Another several minutes passed. The driver, wanting some sign, however indirect, as to what to Adams expected from him next, continued. "I remember visiting here for the first time, as a lad, with my father. He took me to see the World's Fair in, what was it, '88, '89? Could it have been that long ago, Mr. Adams?"

"I'd burn Chartres to the ground before I'd let Her become overrun by tourists, poking around, Baedeker in hand, checking off sights like so many items on a grocery list. Ravaging Her silence. They've already ruined the Mont. I swear I'd set a match to the place before I'd let Her suffer such a fate."

Uncertain how to respond to Adams' outburst, the driver could manage only a "Yes, sir."

"I wish all such cretins would go straight to hell. But no one goes to hell any more, do they? No one believes in hell anymore, do they? No one believes."

"I've never really thought much about it sir. I don't...I don't know."

"But perhaps I do. And perhaps I will...if only to spite them."

Several more minutes of silence ensued. Adams stared at the window. The driver stared down the nave vacantly, once again made uncomfortable by his aged inquisitor. A half a dozen pilgrims stood silently in the midst of the cathedral's labyrinth, as if caught in some sort of occult web. Shadows within the cathedral had perceptibly lengthened when he again spoke.

"They say Mary's mercy is infinite..."

The driver expected a further remark from Adams, but none came. Unconsciously, Adams then began to hum the song he'd heard at lunch. This continued as the light grew dimmer through the windows. The driver raised an eyebrow and stared at the back of his employer's head. Then clearing his throat, he checked his own watch. Several more minutes passed. The ticking of the hands was clearly audible. But eventually the deepening shadows and great silence seemed to muffle even these tiny, clicking assertions of technology. Another several minutes passed.

"They say She embarrassed the schoolmen, humiliated their logic. What do you think, Mr. Foulkestone?"

But there was no reply. Foulkestone had retreated silently to the car some time earlier. Adams had not noticed. It struck him at that moment, though, that the nave's ribs and vaulting suggested he were in the belly of a great fish. He swooned at the thought of being dissolved in the blue, amniotic light which suffused the heights with the last light of day.

Instead, he was spat out. A priest had come up behind Adams and clasped him on the shoulder and told him a memorial service would be beginning shortly in a side chapel and that Adams needed to cease the humming of his song or leave. So Adams left.

During the entire return trip, Adams was hunched over in the backseat of the car, humming and flipping feverishly through Book Eight of the Confessions, the same edition that he'd used as an undergraduate at Harvard years earlier. A quivering patch of light illuminated the text. His eyes ached. Somewhere in the streets of St. Denis, the brittle binding of the old book disintegrated in his hands. Still, he read on. Into the night. Back in his apartment in the Rue Bonaparte, Adams fell asleep quickly and did not awake until noon.

~~~~~~~~~~

Precisely two weeks later, Adams received word that Mueller

would be arriving the next day from Oxford. For the past several weeks their correspondence had increased, with Mueller informing his friend that he believed that he had made significant headway into the mysteries of medieval musical notation and felt certain that Richard's *Song* would soon yield to his relentless pressure. The latest telegram sounded more than hopeful, suggested that perhaps he had indeed deciphered the code. Adams was giddy. His nieces remarked, in whispers among themselves, that they hadn't seen him so excited in years. With Mueller scheduled to arrive in the early afternoon, Adams decided a diversion was needed for the morning unless he should grow too excited thinking about what news his visitor might bring. Miss Tone had again made arrangements for Foulkestone and Adams. The two would drive out to Sacre-Coeur and enjoy a late breakfast at one of Montmartre's cafes. This would give Miss Tone and the others time to prepare for their celebrated guest without having to entertain Adams as well.

When Adams returned at 3:00 PM, he found his old friend seated comfortably in a chair in the converted parlor, conversing animatedly with Adams' nieces, sipping a drink while pivoting about in his other hand a medieval lute he'd taken down from one of the shelves. He set down his glass and the rare instrument, and the two old friends embraced heartily and exchanged greetings. Miss Tone watched from the corner of the room with great pleasure.

After several minutes of lively banter, Adams seated himself beside Mueller and gestured around the room.

"Welcome to my laboratory. A sideshow, really. Nothing more than a social luxury, a conversation piece."

Mueller chuckled and took back up his glass.

"Today, my dear Henry, more than your radiant wit will enliven this room. The notebooks you sent me last month proved beneficial to my research. Little by little, the Middle Ages will be unconcealed. Your work has been most thought provoking."

"That is of course my role, you know, to serve as a gadfly—no, a flea—to my profession. History will die if not agitated. I found that out with my fellow Americans, a flabby, nauseating lot, every one of them. Most of them, anyhow," he said with relish, his eyes twinkling.

Almost in unison, his nieces raised their hands to their mouths to conceal their amusement. Muller nodded his head, a broad smile coming to his face.

"Adams, old friend, it is indeed comforting to see so little has changed." He looked from niece to niece, then set down his drink and held aloft a folder. "But today I bring good news. Good news, my friend, good news! I have here in my possession the answer to our riddle! I hold here in my hands the keys to the kingdom!"

Adams bit his lip in contemplation, a bit confused by the boldness of his friend's claim.

"Your words are slippery, Herr Muller. This wouldn't be another one of your cruel jokes, would it?"

"No joke, my dear Adam. A simple fact."

It was Adams who now looked from niece to niece, seeking verification of his friend's words, some clue as to whether or not this was indeed some sort of prank. But the expressions on their faces revealed that they were as astonished as he.

Adams' eyes glassed over with thought, lost in some great distance, then returned. He spoke very slowly now, and in a tone which struck his auditors as almost vulnerable.

"As much as I hate facts—and have gone to great length my entire life to avoid them—you must tell me precisely what it is you mean."

Mueller smiled sympathetically and shook his head, as if understanding the source of his friend's changed demeanor.

"Your translation of Richard's *Song* was admirable. In fact, I do you an injustice by calling it a translation. What you have done, dear Adams, is resurrect the song in a new language. Today, I tell you, your years of research will be fulfilled. You have not labored in vain. A song unsounded for over five-hundred years will today be heard. The greatest artifact of the Middle Ages has been reclaimed from the maw of time and restored to its beauty. With you as an inspiration, I have spent the last two months collating texts and systematically comparing the sources you sent me. With that, and with a good deal of sleuth work on my own, I have managed to subdue this mystery and bring it to heel. A feat neither Holmes nor Dupin could match. In truth, the mystery has astonished even me. So rare and strange. One of which your beloved Caedmon himself could not have dreamt. But, in truth, it is to you, Adams, to you all credit is due. Your words inspired me to solve the riddle of the *Song's* music. And that I believe—I pray—I have done. Miss Tone, if you will be so kind."

On this cue, she approached the Steinway in the middle of the parlor, in a practiced manner that clearly indicated she had rehearsed her role with Mueller during Adams' lunch at Sacre Coeur. And with her movement, the remainder of Adams' staff entered the room and quietly found seats next to his nieces. Mueller walked slowly over to the piano, and laid before Miss Tone what Adams interpreted to be the sheet music to Richard's *Song*. Adams was nearly overcome with excitement. He had pursued this moment for years, nearly blinded himself with the reading of faded manuscripts, forsaken friends and society for what would soon greet his ears. He had slaved over the lyrics to the song until he felt he had them just right. Then he slaved some more. They had become a part of him, and he knew every line by heart. For a decade he had catechized himself, recalling the fate of the ruined cathedral to chasten any hint of contentment. "Danger lurks in every word," he would repeat to himself, hunched over his documents late at night in his laboratory, utterly convinced that his beloved song would collapse like Beauvais if its translation were not properly proportioned, its materials not carefully selected. Only after years was he satisfied with the translation. But still the song's melody, shrouded in the notation of a lost language, eluded him. Until now.

He felt, too, that he had to commend his friends for the pleasing production they had prepared for the song's revelation. It was splendid, really. The stagecraft was not lost on him. The arrangement in the parlor would provide an admirable setting. The cast of players was itself distinguished. The car, the caves, the windows, they all faded from his mind. The chansons were alive in ways which these others were not. And his role had been second to none in granting them life. He was quickened by the thought of himself as a sort of creator, a faded echo of that first creative act that had once moved across the void. With that thought in mind—and the realization that his place in history might finally be secure—Adams sat back in his chair. Digging a hand into the pocket of his waist coat, he clutched the ticking talisman that alone seemed to bring order and control to the very palm of his hand. He remained completely oblivious to the fact that every eye in the room was now fixed on him. He closed his eyes in preparation for the chanson. At least one niece thought she detected one corner of his mouth curling slightly upward in satisfaction.

And then Miss Tone began to play, slowly, and a bit awkwardly at first, but then with increasing confidence. Mueller, in his fine baritone, began to accompany her.

But they had not even finished the first verse when Adams stoop up and interrupted Mueller's voice with his own, silencing the astonished professor before finishing the verse in perfect pitch, accompanying Miss Tone as if the two had rehearsed the song for months. The room was dumbstruck. When she realized the full significance of what was happening, Miss Tone's playing trickled off into silence. More than one person seated in the parlor thought she'd looked as if she'd seen a ghost. Incredibly, Adams sang three verses of the lyrics, in perfect pitch, according to the precise melody Miss Tone had established. Then he collapsed back into his chair, not fully aware himself of what had happened. A minute of silence passed.

"How the devil, Adams?" Mueller finally asked, still stunned, and even visibly shaken, at how his friend knew the melody and a little embarrassed at being upstaged in front of a crowd.

But Adams said nothing, only slumped back into his chair and stared vacantly across the room. His nieces rushed to his side, fearing the worst. Adams remained silent, as if struck dumb by the very bullet which at the moment was crashing through the head of an archduke half a continent away. He began shaking, and a cold sweat broke out on his brow. Miss Tone rushed out of the room crying to get help. Mueller knelt down beside his old friend and shook his arm.

"Adams, come to old boy, what is it? Are you alright? The *Song* Adams, was it the *Song*? Am I somehow mistaken? Did I miss the mark, old boy, did I miss the *Song*?"

But Adams remained silent. Though the lyrics were Richard's— Adams had spent seven years of labor to insure that was the case—the melody Adams had heard before, sung to him in a cheap cabaret from the lips of a painted whore.

~~~~~~~~~~

Adams did not speak for days. Not even when informed of the

events in Sarajevo. The doctor had concluded it was no stroke but a mild nervous collapse brought on by overexertion. He recommended a week of rest. After some protest, Adams relented. One night late, when Miss Tone had come into Adams' room to check on him, he grabbed her arm and with startling violence pulled her close to him.

"We must leave here now. We must return."

She was too frightened to answer and only nodded he head, then backed away slowly toward the door. She did not mention the incident to anyone.

Initially, there appeared to be no need to do so after all, for in two days, Adams felt better, and, in a week, he was up and about. But the implications of the assassination in Sarajevo soon became clearer over the next few days. The activity in the once bustling apartment on the Rue Bonaparte became noticeably subdued. Ten days later, Foulkestone and Adams were out driving in the Latin Quarter when a policeman stopped and told them that all foreign cars would be impounded soon. Adams nodded his head in silence. Foulkestone turned the car around and headed back to the apartments. Paris had become impossible.

~~~~~~~~~~~

"Miss Tone, you must know by now that I'm a harmless creature. An aged Pierrot, really. All bark. And no bite."

"Yes, Mr. Adams. I'd suspected as much."

Adams smiled. Foulkestone took another sip from his drink and said nothing. This was their third day at sea, and the war was receding into the distance behind them. Only with great fortune had Adams been able to book passage on board the *Rabella* at so late an hour. Not seven days ago he'd learned that the *Cassandra*, the boat he'd originally made reservations for, had been attacked in the North Sea. The ship had staggered on bravely toward Plymouth, hampered by its excessive cargo of goods, a damaged rudder, and a naïve captain. Before leaving the Channel, a torpedo had damaged the engine and hull beyond repair, and the ship foundered at sea without direction for another day before going under not three miles from Southampton. Adams and his coterie had been shocked. A change in plan was necessitated, and it required that only Miss Tone and Mr. Foulkestone accompany Adams on the crossing. The rest of his staff, including two nieces, would take a later boat.

The combination of the probability of the war's escalation and the absence of the company of his nieces had made Adams even more introspective than usual on the first two days of the voyage. But by the third day, he'd begun to loosen up some. Especially after dinner, during which he'd had several drinks. The three had returned to Adams' small cabin for conversation and talked for nearly an hour. Adams remarked caustically on their cramped lodgings and refused to concede that it was not human error, but rather the late reservation caused by the sinking of the *Cassandra*, that was at fault. Miss Tone shook her head and smiled at his stubborn inclination to blame man rather than fate for such occurrences. Foulkestone merely took another sip from his drink. In an attempt to change the topic of conversation, Miss Tone skillfully fashioned a sentence which might segue into talk of either Wilson, Wells, or Kant. Adams fell for the bait and proceeded to hold forth with vigor.

At eleven o'clock, Mr. Foulkestone excused himself and retired to his cabin. He sensed Adams had exhausted his energy. Miss Tone was left alone to prepare Adams' room for sleep. She smiled as he reached nervously for the watch in his pocket, a habit which reminded her of how the washerwomen from the Dingle peninsula of her childhood would finger their rosary beads while at work. He sensed her amusement—that she'd caught him at some sort of mischief—but he was not sure of the offense. Nor did he dwell on it. With Foulkestone gone, Adams resumed talking, seated motionless in the cabin's lone arm-chair.

"You Irish know we Americans are usually unsociable animals, don't you?"

Miss Tone smiled as she pulled back his bed sheets.

"Unsociable and bad at losing. And I've done quite a bit of the latter in my life. Hate it. Did you know, Miss Tone, that it was my lot—my birthright, really—to be the chief failer of my generation, did you know that?"

"Oh, stop your nonsense Mr. Adams. You've never failed at anything at which you've tried."

Adams smiled at the unintended irony of her comment. She continued her work, oblivious to his reaction.

"Looking back on it now, I think Grant had it in for me. He ruined me. I probably helped some, I suppose. It was knowing when to act, really. That was the problem. Always is."

She continued preparing the room, restraining a smile. She'd heard this sort of talk from him on countless occasions.

"Here I am, an old man, after years lost in the archives, plumbing the depths of the past to make sense of the future. An old man, too old to learn a new song, I fear."

"Nonsense Mr. Adams—we're never so old."

He was silent for several minutes before speaking up again. She continued her tasks: preparing his toiletry, placing his glasses on the night stand, setting out his robe, carefully situating his slippers by the bed.

"Do you know what it is to be alone, Miss Tone?"

Now she stopped and turned to face him, for this remark had been spoken in a more desperate, deeply sad, manner. A tone of voice in which she'd never before heard him speak.

"Mr. Adams, I'm here with you. I'll be in the next room the entire voyage. You're not alone. We'll arrive in Boston in a few days."

"Then I'll be more alone."

She had become deeply confused, but she did not want to betray her anxiety. And he continued, almost oblivious to her presence.

"I drew the short straw. And I hadn't even realized we were drawing straws. But, as it turned out, the final watch is mine."

Miss Tone stood motionless. Without words.

"You see, I've buried my wife. My parents. A beloved sister. All my friends. Long ago buried any hope for a son. I've even buried hopes for the nation my family built. Watched them die slow, terrible deaths. I dreamed of great things, Miss Tone. Every day dreamed of great things, Miss Tone. Instead, here I am."

He stopped talking, then looked up into her eyes and continued.

"The only appointment I ever won, Miss Tone, was the one I never wanted. This appointment, this election, this celebrated title which I never sought: to be the lone watcher of the dead."

"Dear Mr. Adams, please don't say such dreadful things."

He was silent for another minute, during which time he placed his pocket watch on the nightstand, just beyond his glasses. She was upset at his remarks but tried to put on a brave front and went to hang up his cardigan.

"The Germans got him too, you know. Augustine, I mean."

She went over to him and helped him to his bed.

"You'll sleep well tonight, and we'll wake up and have a good breakfast."

She said this last remark in an attempt to muster conviction—his and hers. He smiled at her tact.

"You know, Miss Tone, after all these years of struggling against it, I fear I'm in peril of turning Christian. Would that be so horrible? All the others did it, why not me?"

She said nothing.

"Say a little prayer for me tonight, Miss Tone, would you do that?"

"I will, Mr. Adams. And I do so every night."

"Henry."

"I will, Henry."

He smiled at her, touched by her tender revelation.

"You're different from the rest, Miss Tone. I can tell I try their nerves. But you seem to tolerate me. And you even kind of like me, don't you Miss Tone?"

"I do."

He smiled again, amused at her choice of words.

"Promise me one more thing too, Miss Tone. Will you promise me one more thing?"

"Of course, Mr. Adams," she answered, sitting down on the bed next to him.

"Promise me you'll tuck me in, when it's all said and done. Tuck me in nicely, like I did for my generation."

She smiled and pulled the sheets up around him.

"I promise," she said.

"Very well, then. Goodnight, dear."

"Goodnight, Mr. Adams."

Miss Tone gave him a firm pressure on his hand. He struck her at that moment as an ancient child: feeble and hard of hearing yet bright eyed and mischievous. And half aware of something no one else seemed to know of. But only half aware. She smiled warmly into his eyes, extinguished his reading lamp, and left the room. Then

Adams found himself alone in his small, dark cabin. He thought how odd it was that he should at that moment be somewhere in the frigid waters of the North Atlantic, retracing the passage his ancestors had taken years earlier in their search for a way of life that had long since been aborted. The thought unsettled him.

An hour or two of vexed sleep had passed when he suddenly bolted upright. A damp chill had collected on his brow. He strained to listen, thinking he'd heard something coming from outside the cabin's portal. The hypnotic sound of waves. The whistle of wind across the deep, perhaps, or the fading horn of a passing ship. But this sound had struck him as more melodious, like the singsong voice of a youth. Impossible, he thought, unless it were mermaids.

In his confused and groggy state, he reached toward the night-stand for his glasses, but he knocked them to the floor. Cursing beneath his breath, he leaned back across the bed and reached out again, this time for his watch. Clasping it in is hand, he brought it toward him in the darkness and then tried to bring it into focus in the meager light provided by the new moon in the overcast sky.. The watch felt cold. He raised it to his ear and then back. Its ticking had stopped, its hands motionless, stuck at what he thought was 3:16. This made no sense to him, was entirely unaccountable. He desperately shook the watch. And then he froze.

He had suddenly become aware of the quality of a silence which, up to that point in time, was entirely unknown to him. The silence of frozen seafloors. A deafening, amniotic silence. He gasped as if he were at the bottom of a pool and saw shapes moving dimly above him, just beyond his reach. Felt the fear of the child at the very moment he discovers himself lost at the town fair. And then he heard again a faint song. Coming from no direction and every direction.

Terrified, he swore a profane oath and violently shook the watch. Then swore again. And again. The machinery hummed back to life, the momentary suspension of its laws ended. Each tick locked into the next in an endless chain of cause and effect, consonant with an indifferent cosmos. Satisfied, he returned the watch to the nightstand, then lay back down and made effort to listen. To recapture the song. But it had vanished.

There were no mermaids singing to him. In the darkness of his berth, Adams had started with fright, but the quickening—perhaps sensing in him an unreceptive host—departed as suddenly as it had come upon him.

There were no more diversions for Henry Adams. A minute of silence convinced him that beyond the dim glass of the portal there was nothing—only a continent descending into darkness. He shook his head at this realization. Then he lay back down, closed his eyes, and clasping his hands across his chest, wept bitter tears.

Yet beyond the glass and across the waves, a song, indeed, moved on the deep.

A song for Henry Adams.

About the Author

JOHN HUGON PERRYMAN is a fifth generation Texan. He graduated from Greenhill School and Williams College, where he started on the school's first undefeated football team, and then received his PhD from UT Dallas. He has published fiction, poetry, and criticism in a wide range of journals, including *The Southern Humanities Review, The South Carolina Review, Concho River Review, RE:AL,* and *The Midwest Quarterly.*

CPSIA information can be obtained
at www.ICGtesting.com
Printed in the USA
LVHW091415121021
700235LV00005B/319